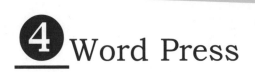

4 Word Press

P R E S E N T S

Behold

A

Pale

Whore

the next episode

A novel by *MARCUS SPEARS*

BEHOLD A PALE WHORE

ISBN: 0-9753966-1-7
Copyright 2005 by Marcus Spears

Published by **4** Word Press

P.O Box 6411
Bridgeport, Connecticut 06606
www.4wordpress.com

Written by Marcus Spears for 4WordPress
First 4Word Press printing 2005
Printed in the United States of America.

For information regarding special discounts for bulk purchases and distribution please contact: (203) 373-1623 or 4 Word Press P.O Box 6411 Bridgeport, Connecticut 06606 or www.4wordpress.com

**Dedicated
To
No Thing
And
No One
But All**

ONE LOVE

4 Word Press

P R E S E N T S

Behold

A

Pale

Whore

the next episode

A novel by *MARCUS SPEARS*

Shout outs

First and foremost I would like to give praise to the Great Mother. To my Wiz Coletta, Moms Donna, and Sun Amun, I love you. R.I.P Auntie Pam. Peace to Uncle Les, Drey, Tae, Tanya, KeKe, Stef, Ivory, La, Meg and Eddie. One.

Spit fire east, west, north and south to my girls Kali, Ma'at, Sekmet, Lilith, Lakshmi, Sophia, Isis, Shu and Nut, Jai Ma! To my mans and them Shiva, Anpu, Heru, Sut, Min, Heru-Khuti, Geb, Tehuti and Amun and all others who dwell inside, ashe'.

To all the bookstores and distributors that pay on time, nuff respect.
Congratulations to brother Sanford from 125th, on his new marriage.

To the 4 Word Press staff, love is the law.

To the alchemical process taking place in the book business, one love. The next generation is here! To all you so called "astute PHD writers" with dusty books on the shelves complaining that your shit ain't selling because of street literature, kiss my ass and write a love story about it!

Last and definitely not least, I thank everyone that copped my books. I cannot thank you enough. One.

Marcus Spears

Mende's Preface

Slowly she emerged from the lucid blue sea onto the hot white sand. The glow surrounding her face resembled the Sun, adjoined with a smile in the shape of a crescent moon. Her body glimmered like a 15 carat diamond as the water dripped from each curve. I glanced with envy finding myself entrenched. My eyes gazed upon her black radiant skin with jealousy, as resentment rushed through my veins like a hot flash. Plastic surgery could never bestow a figure like that. Soon her stride seemed to glide toward me, as if her feet were on casters. The sunshine vanished immediately and the sky became violent with gloomy clouds and roaring thunder. In that instant I recognized Kali's ferocious stare. During a panic attempt to grab the pistol under my beach chair, I froze; it was too late.

"Payback's a bitch BITCH!" Kali uttered charging forward, then "*WWWSSSHHH*," her blade made a slicing sound through the wind before it slashed my throat.

The bleeding wouldn't stop and my head started spinning in delirium. My whole life played out before me in what felt like seconds. I couldn't believe I was going out like this. My eyes closed shut then everything faded as I fell sideways in the sand.

Even though I was only dreaming, I awoke as if everything had actually happened. The bed sheets were soaked with sweat and the warm menstrual blood in the center caused me to panic even more.

"No! Stop! Nooooo!" I jumped out of bed swinging my arms in a wild rage, struggling to snap out of it.

"It's all right honey, it's okay. You're having a nightmare again" my newlywed husband reassured, "Just relax and take deep breaths" he said as he coached me back to sanity.

This disturbing revelation of being murdered at the hands of someone I betrayed haunted me every night for two weeks straight now. I was supposed to be enjoying my new life without looking back at the past, but I couldn't stop thinking about Kali. I knew she would track me down to settle the score because revenge is her attribute. Between all the crimes I committed, and countless number of people whom I backstabbed, it was a miracle that I lived long enough to even ponder the past. They say we all have to pay for the things we do in life and lately I've been feeling like my time was closing in.

While my husband ran a hot bubble bath for me, I rolled up a nice fat blunt. Each morning before dawn, I usually swam naked in the ocean to calm my nerves, but I was scared to go outside now in fear that my nightmare would come to pass. Instead, I soaked in the hotel's spacious tub puffing away like Bob Marley with cucumber slices over my eyelids. The Purple Haze began to take effect. Drama filled memories played out in my mind as the bubbles dissolved into the water. My thoughts drifted back to the ninth grade, the point where it all started and how everything in life began to change.

Scene One:

The jump off

Before I explain how a white girl like me got involved with a group of militant black females from New York City, I have to start from the beginning. I wasn't always a nigger loving cokehead. On the contrary, I was much the prissy xenophobe, until rap music hit the suburbs. Yo MTV! Raps and BET, set off a strong desire in me to look and dress like a hood chick. There was even a stronger desire in me to screw their boyfriend's brains out. In all honesty I can't stand those black motherfuckers now, but back in the day I would have done just about anything to get my mouth on some chocolate.

Most people knew me as Patricia Gubenhimer, until I adopted the name Mende from one of my father's ancient books on sex and sorcery. Flipping through the pages I learned about the goat of Mendes, a rebellious erotic trickster also known as Baphomet. Since I loved giving rise to lust and passion too, the name fit me well. I even had its symbol, an inverted five-pointed star, tattooed on the back of my thigh. While reading *The Secret Teachings of All Ages* more carefully, I found out this symbol was mostly used in the practices of magick. In some places it was even called the footprint of the devil, but so what. My father wanted me to have the tattoo removed, so to piss him off even more I had my tongue pierced. Mind you I was only 13 when all this took place.

Growing up with a promiscuous older sister gave me the privilege of learning how to use my tongue ring and other skillful sex techniques. Whenever her boyfriends came by, I would hide in the closet with her permission and watch them get busy. In view of strange looking black dudes corking my sister with cock, a mushroom cloud of lust detonated in my crotch.

Eventually I got tired of just watching and started roaming the streets in search of my own big black dick to ride. Mentally I preferred grown men in their late twenties or so, with wives and kids at home, not little boys my own age. Yet once I started having sex, age was no longer an issue for me. As long as a man could get it up, I could put it down, no matter how old or young they were.

On a warm spring day after soccer practice there he was, my first official piece of dark meat. His name was Jamal, a nice looking black guy who worked for the Parks & Recreation department. I had my eye on him for some time now and although Jamal was three times my age, he wore his uniform in a stylish manner that made him appear much younger than he actually was. Jamal's fitted Yankee caps were always tilted 45 degrees to the left, with a doo-rag underneath and I loved the way his gold chains sat between his curved-in pectoral muscles.

Like any other landscaper would do, Jamal cut the grass and took care of the surrounding fields where our high school soccer team practiced. I had a better job in store for his fine black ass. During each practice I ran up and down the grassy turf in my sexy uniform skirt. Sometimes it would blow up revealing my thong underwear, if I wore any at all. Jamal always shot a glance my way, as he rode alongside the fence on his lawn mower. I figured the sneak peek of my cheeks turned him on, so I would slowly lick my lips whenever we made eye contact.

A short distance away from the school was a puny supply shack where Jamal kept his tools and stuff. So while the rest of the team hit the showers, I drifted down the hill one day to pay Jamal a little visit. To my advantage I strolled in on him smoking a joint. Jamal had his size 14 boots plopped up on a tool-infested desk, while he blew smoke through his nostrils like a dragon.

"Can I help you" Jamal coughed, as he brushed ash from his shirt.

"We're finally alone" I spoke softly as I walked up to him, "I seen the way you look at me Jamal, and I can tell that you want some of this don't you?"

"Some of what?" Jamal questioned oddly with his eyes red as hell.

"Some of this!" I answered, now standing at arms length.

To Jamal's surprise I unsnapped my skirt then lowered my white lace panties with both thumbs. My youthful bush was exposed, but Jamal backed away as if my pussy stank.

"Hey little girl I don't know what you think you're doin', but you betta' stop it before I-"

"Before you what nigga!" I raised my tone as I moved in closer, "tell on me?"

Locking eyes with Jamal, I slowly passed my hand over his chest then said, "I'm not the one getting high on the clock, so if you want to keep this corny ass job of yours, I suggest you give me what I want or I'll scream rape."

Jamal looked at me like I was crazy then pushed me out of the way. Brushing me aside only riled my temper, so I ran to the exit screaming, "HELP ME! HELP ME! Some black man on drugs is trying to touch me!"

It was all a put on, because I knew no one could hear me all the way from the supply shack, but Jamal didn't know if I was serious or not. He covered my mouth with his large coarse hands as he aggressively pulled me back inside the door. I liked playing ruff, and the more he took control, the more I became aroused. My hole began to heat up like grease in a frying pan and I could even feel my clitoris tingle in anticipation of getting what I came for.

"I'll slap the shit outta' you if you don't stop yellin' that bullshit!" Jamal shouted while he shook the hell out of me, "are you crazy girl?"

All of a sudden Jamal let go. His voice faltered then he held his head in his hands.

"*If I lose another job*" he thought out loud, "*my P.O is gonna' violate me for sure...I'm not goin' back to jail over some horny lil' white bitch fuck that!*"

"You don't have to go to jail or lose your job, if you whip it out for me" my voice purred and eyes twinkled.

"Why you gotta' fuck wit' me?" Jamal asked as he continued to fret.

I never answered Jamal's question, but to myself I was saying, "*Dude! If your feet are that big I can't wait to see the size of your cock! That's why I'm fucking with you!*"

I had Jamal right where I wanted. Since he was on parole at the time, Jamal needed his $8 dollar an hour job to stay out of prison and feed his family. He knew that if I accused him of fondling me people would believe my story, rather than take the word of a two-time felon. Either way Jamal would get fired, so without any enthusiasm he unzipped his blue Dickie uniform slacks. His facial expression was just as lifeless as his dangling penis. It was obvious that he didn't want to really fuck me, so I dropped to my knees to give him some incentive.

I licked the length of his floppy dick until it began to swell. In no time a ramrod filled my mouth as I jerked and pulled. I could barely get my hands around that big thing, so I used both hands and sucked it some more until my jaw became sore. Given that Jamal was so well endowed, I was afraid that his pussy-pounder was going to hurt. Like a truck driver cautiously backing into a loading dock, I carefully backed onto Jamal. *Beep-Beep-Beep-Beep.*

Aching bliss was the only pain to be felt. My sopping wet vagina slid tightly around his thick dick as I whimpered with delight, "oh yeah nigga that's it push it all the way."

From the way I rotated my hips, Jamal could no longer pretend to be uninterested.

"Damn it's so hot and tight," he moaned before bending me over a chair.

I knew it felt good, because he put his back into it like every man should. With my eyes closed I bit down on my lip as he started to pump. The sound of Jamal's balls slapping against my ass sped up as he proceeded to rabbit fuck me. I screamed with pleasure the faster he plowed my coochie like a beast.

"Oh my god! Yes! Yes!" I howled in ecstasy, "I'm gonna' cum, I'm gonna' cum!"

Seconds later I came or better yet, I

arrived! I kneeled before Jamal like he was a priest and I was a parishioner receiving communion. My tongue was out at full length and with one eye shut I prepared for a hot blast.

When I stood up to swap fluids with Jamal, he pulled my hair back like he was going to kiss me at first. Instead he hog spit down my throat before shoving my face to the floor.

"You got it twisted" Jamal sneered, "I don't kiss filthy hoes! Now get the fuck out'a here!"

The blood in my veins pulsated. I was energized and his disrespect only turned me on. I felt too relieved to get mad at that point, because I got what I wanted, so I wiped the droplets of sperm from my mouth then snapped my skirt back on before leaving.

"Was it as good for you as it was for me?" I taunted walking away.

"Fuck you and your flat ass bitch!"

Apart from Jamal's comment about my ass, I still felt powerful as ever. In the same way as my ancestors used their slaves for sex, I too had conquered a black man. Although I never fucked Jamal again after our little episode, I bet he still thinks about the 14-year-old white girl who pimped him like one of Willie Lynch's daughters.

The next day I sat Indian style on my bedroom floor as a teammate braided my hair. The phone rang, but I could barely hear it over the old Biggie album we blasted.

"Yo nigga hand me the phone before my

father picks it up" I hollered over the backdrop of *Juicy*.

"I don't work here" Tasha retorted with an attitude, "and don't be using the N word around me like that either!" She said, as she pulled my braid tighter.

As soon as I picked up the phone I knew exactly who it was.

"*This is a collect call from the Webster Correctional facility-* from [MANNY]" the automated operator instructed, before Manny's actual voice interrupted, "*to accept this call say yes after the tone.*"

"Hell no!" I screamed into the receiver before slamming the phone down.

"Damn who was that you just shit on?" Tasha asked.

"Your boy Manny...he's a pain in the ass!" I replied.

All types of guys called me, but not that many from prison. It seemed like Manny wasn't even locked up, seeing how frequently he called. From the one time when I talked dirty to Manny while he jerked off over the phone, he hadn't stopped calling me collect since. What good is a man behind bars? What could Manny's locked up, *can you please send me a money order*, begging ass do for me?

"What's he callin' your house for anyway?" Tasha interrogated before finishing the last line of cornrows, "I told you Manny got a baby by my cousin...let her find out you messin' around wit' her man and she will fuck you up quick!"

"ILK! I don't want his ugly ass" I responded defensively, "she could have 'em!"

Even though I was the type of chick to make you think your man is ugly then fuck 'em the first chance I got, in Manny's case he was really ugly. I truly could care less about him.

"Trust me Tasha the last thing on my mind is Manny" I smiled devilishly, "while you and the rest of the team hit the showers after practice yesterday, I was down the hill gettin' my freak on."

"You're such a liar Mende" Tasha rolled her eyes, "I was with you almost all day yesterday."

"Not after practice you weren't. Remember that cute guy who cuts the grass? The one who I said looks at me like he wants to blow my back out?"

"Yeah Jamal the maintenance man?" Tasha shrieked with skepticism and excitement.

"Yeah the big long maintenance man" I answered wetting my lips, "I finally got my chance to Lil' Kim his ass" I said as I examined my hair in the mirror singing, "*Take it in the butt...wha' what!*"

Sharing the juicy details with Tasha seemed to offend her, but fuck Tasha. She was a crumb from the projects.

"Patricia is that a cigarette I smell?" My father hollered from the hallway, "And who was that on the phone?" He asked, now standing outside of my door, "The caller I.D read Webster

Correctional?"

"Nobody dad, wrong number" I lied.

"What's that smell?" My father queried, as he tried to open my door.

"Nothing! I was just burning incense," I replied sourly with my foot blocking the door, "can I get dressed in private please!"

"Well you girls are going to be late for practice if you don't hurry up."

"Aw'right, we'll be down in a minute" I chuckled while dying out my cigarette.

After tossing the empty beer bottles and blunts under my bed, we ran down the stairs and hopped in the car.

My father was strict and hated black people for the most part, but for some reason he didn't mind me hanging out with Tasha. Although daddy was a known racist, his favorite athletes and musicians were all black. Since Tasha was the school's star athlete, I guess that's why he liked her so much.

"How's my favorite goalie?" Daddy asked as soon as we got in the car, "why don't you sit up front with me Tasha? We can talk about last week's game."

"No that's okay Mr. G I'm fine back here with Patricia" Tasha made a face at me like my father was buggin'.

If I didn't know better I would have swore that my father had a hard-on. He kept fixing the rear view mirror to get a look at her legs and even smiled at everything she said. The look in his eye was familiar to me. It was the same look I displayed when I seen something I wanted to taste.

Tasha wasn't from the wealthy suburbs of Wallingford like I was; she was from the poor inner city of New Haven. Last year my school was charged with being a racist establishment, because it's black student enrollment was at a whopping 2%. Minority leaders publicized this fact, which compelled the $3000 a month institution to set up a voucher system. They bussed in black students from surrounding areas and based on her outstanding athletic ability, Tasha made the list.

I envied Tasha even though I was the one who was chauffeured to school everyday, lived in a big fancy house and wore expensive clothes all the time. To this day I don't know why I was so envious of her, but there is something about pretty black girls that makes me jealous for no reason. It would be fair to say that I bought Tasha's friendship. The only reason Tasha bothered with me was because every week I paid her good money to braid my hair in cornrows. Sometimes I would give her a little extra, if she let me hang out with her in the hood.

The white picket fence lifestyle was mundane to me and I enjoyed chilling in the run down sections of New Haven, because it made me feel cooler than the rest of the white girls I knew. At the moment I didn't realize how silly I looked rocking blonde cornrows and big gold earrings with my name in the middle.

Originally I thought black people were just thugs and drug dealers like television portrayed, but the ones Tasha introduced me to were decent hard working people. My father used to always say that niggers were nothing more than lazy porch monkeys living off of taxpayer's money, but Tasha made it clear to me that statistically there were more white people collecting welfare than blacks.

For a housing project, Tasha's area was quiet.

"I wanna' see some real hood action" I said to Tasha as we walked to her house one day, "you know...like a drive-by or a drug deal or something gangsta' like that."

"How 'bout I punch you in the face then sell you some Advil for the headache afterwards?" Tasha sucked her teeth, "This ain't a fuckin' zoo tour bitch! Just cause we're poor don't mean we ain't civilized."

In my opinion I found the wild niggas more interesting. If they weren't ruff and thugged out, I wouldn't waste my time.

Tasha and I were both 14, but she had a thick grown woman's shape and a sense of pride that made her stand out amongst the rest. Whenever we were together men always came up to Tasha first. If she dissed them, then they tried to talk to me, since I was the only remaining option. I got tired of that shit. I wanted niggas to willingly approach me for pussy when I stepped my ass in the projects, forget having to throw it in their faces like a desperate crack head begging to get laid.

As time went by I became more familiar with the hood and learned what was hot and what was not. Material wise I had the look down pat. I copied Tasha's whole style from the slang she used down to the ditty in her bop, but nothing I did made me desirable like she was. I wore all the expensive name brand clothes and accessories featured in the hip-hop magazines, but physically I was still lacking something. Black men liked their girls thick with ass and the only things thick on my body were my calves from playing soccer. Standing next to Tasha made my body look like a pancake. Everything about her was natural, but that didn't mean I had to be.

I laid on my bed looking through old pictures the day my junior year of high school came to an end. Unfortunately Tasha would not be returning to Wallingford Prep next year, because her parents could not keep up with the reduced, but still steep tuition. Most likely she would wind back up in her old high school. So anyway, while I was staring at this 4x7 picture of Tasha and I in our spandex gymnastic uniforms, it hit me.

"Implants..."

The shapes that her body flaunted gave me the notion to get breast implants and other cosmetic surgery. All my white girlfriends were getting it done and I didn't know why I didn't think about this earlier. With a little nip here and a tuck there, I could have a figure like Tasha's after all! Whoever said money can't buy you everything must have been a broke motherfucker.

I daydreamed about all the boys at school falling to my feet in admiration of my new curves. But first I had to convince my father somehow that I needed ten thousand bucks for a makeover. I called my sister in California who had her tits done a month ago, for advice and information. Jenny explained to daddy over the phone that it was common for girls my age to get nose jobs or tummy tucks or whatever cosmetic surgery they needed to improve their self-confidence. She described how important it was for a girl to feel good about herself, but didn't mention anything about me actually getting breast implants until the end of the conversation.

The answer was no. My father didn't go for it and said that he wasn't paying any lousy doctor to make his daughter look like a porno star. He told Jenny when I turn 18 and have my own money, I could do whatever I want to do to my body, but until then, the answer was still no.

I didn't give a shit what my father said. I never listened to him before, so why would I start listening to him now. My ass was getting surgery no matter what I had to do to get the money.

Scene Two:

Shake what the doctor gave ya'

Like every summer off from school I packed my bags to visit relatives out in California. Typically I despised flying hours just to mingle with phony acting family members who barely knew me, but this time I would be traveling for a good reason. My brother Chad, who usually accompanied me on the trip, couldn't make it this year thank god. He and my father were in the middle of fighting some legal battle back home.

The best part of all was that my sister Jenny agreed to set up everything for me for a little favor. She happened to be dating one of California's top plastic surgeons, who would hook me up if I hooked her up. Naturally I agreed. Where else was I going to get the $10,000 it would cost for the operation?

During the majority of the flight we were hit with major turbulence. I was a nervous wreck, guzzling little bottles of Gin while reading about the pros and cons of cosmetic surgery. Before landing in Los Angeles I managed to sneak in the last few sips as I exited the plane. In the wake of claiming my baggage, I walked out of LAX airport with authentic Louis Vuitton logo luggage at my side. My appearance was that of the average white girl on vacation and no one knew that I had over $250,000 worth of drugs in my bag.

Jenny was waiting outside the airport. She welcomed me with an ice-cold Corona and a lit cigarette. In return I greeted her with the same fake ass kiss on the cheek and kept it moving. My sister hadn't changed at all. Jenny was the same money hungry floozy that she was before college.

"You got my shit?" Jenny asked right away, "cause if you don't you can hop your ass right back on the plane."

"It's in my bag bitch damn, can I at least get in the fuckin' car first!"

I handed over five perfume-sized bottles of fluid after flicking my cigarette to the ground. The favor I owed was simple. All I had to do was smuggle some designer drugs on the plane and everything after that would be taken care of. I felt the chances of getting caught by airport security were slim, because who would search a little innocent looking white girl like me.

"Guess how much money these little bottles are worth?" Jenny stared in awe as she held one of the glass containers between her finger and thumb, "fifty big ones a piece baby!

"What type of weird shit are you into these days?" I questioned strangely, "Fifty gees? It looks like a little bottle of piss to me."

Even though Jenny was wild and all that, she still had a strange geeky side. In high school she sold her estrogen to fertile clinics just to buy a leather dress my father refused to get for her. There was no telling what that stuff was in those bottles.

"Obviously you don't keep up with the latest trends my dear...its DMT" Jenny stated simply.

I looked at her expressionless like I was supposed to really know what that was.

"Daddy's an undertaker and you never heard of Dimethyltryptamine? It's brain fluid stupid!"

I didn't know what in the hell she was talking about, but played along like I understood. Jenny put in plain words that my brother Chad, who worked as an anesthesiologist, unlawfully extracted spinal fluid from pregnant women during their epidural procedures. He then mixed it with Dimethyltryptamine pineal fluid that he took from dead bodies in my father's mortuary. Jenny then sold the precious extract all over California to wealthy actors and musicians for big doe. It was the new craze in Hollywood and her doctor friend loved the shit.

"I'm not gonna' waste my time explaining to an idiot like you every medical detail of how and why it happens," Jenny flipped her hair back, "but when DMT is injected into the blood stream you can experience the genetic memory of the person it was extracted from as it enters your Hypothalamus gland...wanna' try some?"

"Sure. Does daddy know about this?" I asked while scanning the parking lot to see if anyone was nearby as Jenny carefully filled a syringe.

"Why do you think he's being sued? Daddy's been selling body parts for years." Jenny made a face, "okay just be still this is gonna' pinch a little."

Jenny placed the needle to my forearm crease as I held a tourniquet around my bicep to pop out a vein. I looked away in repulsion as she carefully injected the dose of DMT into my blood stream. In seconds I was nodding like a dope fiend, experiencing the most euphoric high ever. It felt like I entered another person's mind. When we pulled off in her boyfriend's Aston Martin, Jenny downed her Corona while the summer breeze blew through her luxurious blonde hair. Since Jenny was into heavy metal nowadays, she blasted her favorite headbanger CD the whole time we zoomed 100mph down the expressway.

Originally I was supposed to stay with my

grandmother in Beverly Hills like my father wanted, but I would have rather slept on a goddamn park bench than spend another fucking summer with Grandma's old musty crypt keeper looking ass. Some of Jenny's friends had already started a bonfire near the shoreline by the time we pulled up to her crib. They were jumping around having fun, drinking like hooligans at a hockey game.

I felt exhausted in need of some rest, but Jenny happened to be throwing a party at her new beachfront condo in Santa Monica that night. Sleeping was out of the equation. Everyone except me was dressed straight out of an Abercrombie & Fitch catalog. They all wore dingy looking T-shirts with filthy flip-flops, as if it was stylish to look dirty. My clean hip hop style of dress didn't fit in, but in the midst of strangers chugging down beers and smoking weed, I eventually socialized instead of crashing on the couch.

When I woke up the next morning I had a throbbing headache. The 151 vodka shots and garbage weed I smoked gave me a fucking migraine. Empty beer bottles and grease stained pizza boxes were left everywhere and I even had to kick my way through trash just to get to the bathroom. I stared into the mirror for twenty minutes examining my unsightly body. The huge mirrors and big bulb dressing room lights that decorated Jenny's bathroom, revealed every detailed flaw on my skin. I felt so ugly that I couldn't even look at myself for too long.

"Mommy has a big surprise for you two" I spoke softly to my A-cup size tits like they were kids, "soon mommy will be able to kiss you good night."

After washing up quickly I got dressed excited for my big day. I had a bag already packed with all the essentials one would want to have with them for a short stay in the hospital.

"Jenny wake up I don't wanna' be late. Jen-nieee...wake up wake up wake uhhup" I whined, while jingling her car keys next to her ear.

"What time is it?" Jenny snatched the keys from my hand with her eyes still closed, "just give me five more minutes I'm begging you please."

My appointment was scheduled for 9 A.M and I wanted to get there early. After forcing Jenny to brush her teeth, she slid on her Gucci slippers and we hit the highway. Whereas most people drank coffee in the morning to get going, Jenny had another way of perking up. She drove slowly down Wilshire Boulevard in Beverly Hills sniffing lines of coke in between sentences.

Jenny tried talking me out of getting large implants even though she had just got her already huge implants re-enlarged two months ago. I wasn't listening to a word she said. I was too nervous that the police were going to pull us over and just nodded like a bobble head doll the entire time.

"Well this is it" I took a deep breath as we walked into the fancy looking doctors office.

Since it was still early we were the only people there besides the doctor and his staff. Jenny sat with me in the waiting room flipping through photo albums of previous patients to get an idea of what breast sizes would look best on me. I didn't need her stank breath opinion and ignored her once again.

"You must be the lovely Patricia" said Doctor Crowley, while I sat there scanning the Essence best sellers list, "Jenny has told me so much about you" he said, "why don't you come with me so we can go over some preliminary measures."

Jenny had been sleeping with this 40-yr old doctor for months. He wasn't the most handsome guy in the world, but he was a board certified plastic surgeon, know what I'm saying? If I knew my sister well enough, she was only fucking his brains out for the perks. Who wouldn't like trips to Hawaii for lunch and shopping sprees on Rodeo drive every week?

Doctor Crowley acted so mannerly in front of his staff, but when he closed the office door his whole style changed. One minute he's acting like Mr. Rogers, than the next he's acting like John Gotti.

"You got my shit?" Doctor Crowley asked as soon as the door shut, "'cause if you don't you can walk your ass right out this office."

"It's in my bag Al. Relax, honey."

In exchange for the bottles Jenny handed over, Doctor Crowley handed me some paperwork to sign, which I happily did.

"Now that we're all settled you can come this way" he winked after squeezing my behind with both hands, "I'll have you prepped and ready to go in no time."

I showed Doctor Crowley the picture I kept of Tasha to explain how I wanted to look before stripping down to nothing in the examination room.

"I want my shape better than hers..."

Ten minutes later after the nurses sterilized my entire body, Doctor Crowley rolled me into the operating room. I laid on the gurney table ready for a complete transformation.

"We'll cut here and over here," he spoke to his staff, while using a surgical marker to line the first incision.

"You won't feel a thing miss Gubenhimer just relax and take a deep breath," said the nursing assistant when she placed the anesthesia gas mask to my face, "think happy thoughts and when you open your eyes you'll look absolutely wonderful."

Scene Three:

Daddy dearest

I slept hours after the operation and felt groggy and dizzy when I came to. My curiosity and excitement gave me the strength to make it to a Mirror. I couldn't stop smiling at what I observed as I stood in the lavatory saying goddamn to myself! My chest jumped from a mosquito bite A-cup, to a voluptuous 38-DD. My new melons were so perfectly round and succulent now. I expected strangers to approach me in the supermarket asking if they could feel and squeeze them. If they were cute enough I probably would let them do it too.

Prior to surgery my lips were thin and dry looking, but gratefully the collagen shots inflated them to the likeness of Angelina Jolie's luscious porno mouth. There was a lot of soreness and numbing pain to endure, but a few Vitamin C tablets and Pineapple extract stopped the swelling in no time. See as a youngster, I was duped into believing that men liked slim trim blonde gals with small lips and slender bottoms, however hanging out in the projects with Tasha quickly changed that belief. I hadn't seen a black woman yet, with a weave and a big bubble ass lack attention or suffer with any dating problems.

Big booty bitches seemed to mesmerize niggas. I wanted men to gawk at my ass too. I wanted them to shift their crotches and snap their necks like they did when those thick chocolate girls walked pass. For that reason I decided to have the state of the art gluteoplasty (butt enhancement) preformed, regardless of its yearly upkeep. If I had to have other people's beef stuffed in my body just to have a badunkadunk, than that's what I had to do.

Women much older than me came into Crowley's office to get liposuctions and tummy tucks, but he actually filled me up with their unwanted fat cells. I know it sounds nasty but according to research, using human fat was the safest and most natural implant to get for a gluteoplasty. I even read some brochures in the doctor's office that surprisingly gave a complete history of the black woman's rotund derriere. I learned that African women with *Steatopygia*, a condition of particularly protuberant buttocks, were even envied centuries ago all throughout Europe. Their shocking curves caused much discussion and back then, any fashionable white woman wore a bustle skirt just to give off the appearance that she was holding junk in her trunk like African chicks were. So basically I was just repeating history by trying to mimic Tasha.

Anyhow, Doctor Crowley filled each cheek with 5000cc of pure fat, which is about 10 pounds in total added to my backside. Before the stunning enhancement my butt was somewhat flat and boyish, but now I could compete with any video chick in a rump shaker contest and win. There was only one catch to the whole thing.

"At your young age" the doctor warned, "it's more than likely that your body will reabsorb the new fat cells. You'll have to get annual refills to keep up its plump appearance."

For the rest of the summer I let my aching body recoup. Basically I read street novels and shopped online everyday, since none of my bras and draws fit anymore. I used to take a size 8 in jeans, but now my new rump demanded a 14.

My last two days in California were spent shopping on Rodeo drive and working on my tan. I preferred wearing brands like Baby Phat and Rocawear, but ended up buying Gucci and Roberto Cavalli. As much as I wanted to flaunt my new body on the sand, I had no choice but to hit the tanning salon, because I sunburned easily. The artificial sunrays at the tanning salon darkened my chalky white skin a little, but left me with more of an orangey type of appearance.

There was no way I could go back home looking like a freaking carrot, so Jenny took me to the most posh day spa in Beverly Hills to get a Mystic tan. Instead of using artificial light, this place sprayed my entire body with melatonin paint, which gave my skin a tone of light bronze.

"What'chu think Jen," I spun around after the cashier handed back my father's credit card, "do I look fucking hot or what!"

"That shit sucks" Jenny clicked off her cell phone and shook her head in disbelief.

"What's wrong? You think I'm too dark?" I frowned.

"No you look great...it's not you at all, it's daddy. That was Chad on the phone. He said they lost the case."

"So what?" I shook my shoulders like I didn't care, "forget about daddy and let's finish shopping!"

"What do you mean *so what*? Those people were suing daddy for over a million dollars. You better act more concerned than so what, cause that means you're broke now, stupid!"

Besides having to pay the 1.3 million in punitive damages for accidentally cremating a few bodies that were supposed to be embalmed, Chad said the judge also ordered a further criminal investigation into my father's business affairs.

Realizing how serious this was I started crying. Jenny was more nonchalant, because all of her things, like the new condo and tuition were paid for already. I didn't even own a car yet and basically lived off of my father's credit cards.

"What am I gonna' do?" I sniveled, in between wiping tears from my lip.

"Well at least you got new tits!" Jenny teased, as she bobbled my breasts, "*I can see it now* we can make a fortune in Vegas as *the titty twins.*"

"Do you think grandma would help daddy out with some money if he asked?" I questioned in desperation.

"Hell no after what happened to mommy" Jenny smirked, "I don't think so. Grandma blames him for mommy's death...I'm just glad I moved out of Connecticut when I did."

At one time my father was one of the wealthiest morticians in Connecticut until his heavy drinking destroyed his reputation. Marrying my mother resuscitated his business, but when she died her blue blood money left with her.

I was supposed to feel good boarding the plane with my new look and all, but I felt depressed and stressed. There was no way I could live as a broke motherfucker for the rest of my life. No way. After landing safely at Tweed airport I waited almost two hours for my father to pick me up. When he finally got there I was in the middle of writing down this dude's phone number and he flipped.

"I'm going to tell you this once and once only" he reprimanded while yanking me through the Airport, "if I catch you talking to one of those head rag niggers again you'll be sorry! Do you understand me Patricia!"

"Whatever daddy why you trippin'?" I sucked my teeth when he ripped the phone number up in my face, "we were just talking damn!"

Daddy didn't say a word about my obvious enhancements or even ask me how my vacation or flight was. He was in a real bad mood and it showed. I hadn't seen him get upset like this in years. As we were waiting at a light this hooked up Mercedes pulled up alongside of us blasting Usher.

"I don't know what happened to this country" my father heaved a sigh, "Niggers used to shine shoes for a nickel and tap dance for a penny, now look at those sons a bitches in their fancy cars. I'm disgusted with everything...listen I have to start clamping down on spending Patricia, so I cancelled most of my credit cards and we have to probably move soon too."

"Why dad? Did you lose the house?"

"*Those goddamn courts and their laws*" he thought out loud as the Benz pulled off, "No, but I have to sell the house or they'll take it from me."

"Am I still going to Prep?" I asked, hoping the answer was no.

"For now you're not, but that's only until I get back on my feet...I just can't afford it right now."

By the time September came around to go back to school we were living in a neglected section of New Haven. My father sold the house in Wallingford along with some other property he owned, just to pay off the lawsuit. Our new location in New Haven was nice, if you like sharing space with dead bodies. One of my father's friends gave him a good price on an old crematory/funeral home, so he took it in hope of starting his business all over again.

My pride was shattered I must say, but New Haven was nothing like Wallingford. Never could I purchase a bag of weed in the same store where I bought toilet paper and pads. Be careful what you wish for sometimes you might get it. Unlike my old hood, where black people were rarely seen outside after dark, niggas in New Haven actually stood on the corners playing loud music until all hours of the night. Gunshots rang out on a regular basis and many times I heard people running through our backyard escaping the police.

My father's pockets were in no position to argue about where to send me to school, so I won over the decision to enroll in Hill House High. Opposite to Wallingford Prep, Hill House had a demographics ratio of 2% white. I knew Tasha was going there and I couldn't wait to see the look on her face when she seen how big my tits and ass got.

Two words could only describe Hill House: Chocolate paradise. Being the new pussy in school pulled all the guys attention when I got off the bus, so I expected bitches to throw salt in my game. I seen some other chicks in the hall with nice behinds and natural double D's, but regardless of what they had I was gonna' work my sex magic like a wizard.

When I spotted Tasha talking with some friends down the hall, I waved so she could see me.

"Yo Tasha what up, come holla' at ya' girl!" I shouted.

I was really excited to see her again, but it took Tasha some time to acknowledge me. When she finally came over to where I stood, it was almost time for class.

"What'chu doin' here?" Tasha asked, "why ain't you in Prep with all the other rich hoes?"

Tasha's friends surrounded me like they wanted to jump me or something.

"I thought that was you I saw getting off the bus this morning" Tasha snickered, "what happened to the Benz? What happened to *I'll never take a bus cause that's for poor people* Mende?"

Tasha really sounded bitter. I couldn't understand why she was trying to ridicule me after all the money I gave her to braid my hair and show me around the hood.

"What's up with you Tasha? Why you acting like them?" I rolled my eyes at the pack standing behind her.

"Them!" One of Tasha's friends started a

racial uproar, "What's *them* mean bitch...black people?"

"*We should fuck this white bitch up!*" the small crowd roared.

The next thing I know somebody punched me in the face before the security guard broke everything up. Tasha walked away without saying anything else to me. I found out later that the girl who hit me was Tasha's cousin. She was the one that happened to be messing around with Manny when he was calling my house from prison.

"Oh its like that T?" I stood alone waiting for an answer, "It's like that! I thought we were sisters."

"I guess so" she replied as the crowd dispersed and everyone else walked back to class, "sisters don't try to fuck each other's man slut! Leave Tariq the hell alone or I'll punch you in the face myself!"

"*I let her black ass come to my house and eat my food and talk on my phone and she got the nerve to act like she's better than me now?* I mumbled to myself, "*I'll fix her black ass watch!*"

When I got off the bus earlier that morning, I ran into this blazin hottie. His name was Tariq and I met him in the projects while hanging out with Tasha. I didn't know that he and Tasha were currently going out, so when I spotted him we hugged and kicked it. Someone must have seen us hug and told Tasha that I was all up in her man's face.

It was true that I wanted to freak Tariq since the first day we met, but I never pushed up on him out of respect. But since Tasha tried to play me around her little friends, I felt like fuck respect now!

With balloon size tits and a fat ghetto booty, I knew I could scoop Tariq with the quickness. Tariq and I shared most of the same classes, so we were able to converse plenty. After talking on the phone for a couple of months, I enticed Tariq to ditch his last two periods and sneak with me to my crib. On the way over there Tariq confessed that he was a virgin. He said that Tasha made him wait 4 months before she even let him feel on her breasts. When he said that, the thought of fresh meat popped into my mind, and I licked my lips like a vampire getting ready to taste new blood.

It was obvious to me that Tariq's only reason for skipping school was to break his virginity, but who cares about feelings when you just wanna get in a nigga's pants. Given the fact that so many black chicks thought blow jobs were nasty and acted stingy with their mouths, I got hip to the head game early on in life and have been swallowing logs ever since. Granting good head was a secret us white girls from the suburbs used to steal inner-city cats away from their women. I learned from watching my sister.

"The key is to make it wet" Jenny shared her expertise, *"spit on it like you're mad if you have to and always make loud slurping noises*

while you suck...men love that shit!"

As soon as we got to the basement I ripped open my shirt. Tariq was in amazement at how big my breasts were now from the first time we met. I let him ogle for a minute, before pulling his head into my chest. Tariq got so hard, that I thought his dick was going to shoot off from his body and fly around the room like a rocket. I teased him, slowly licking his meat like a chocolate icicle, then slobbered away as I played with myself at the same time.

"Who was that? You said nobody was home?" Tariq whispered in concern as my head went up and down, "Is somebody upstairs?" He nervously asked.

Suddenly the basement door flew open. The rapid bang of the door slamming against the wall startled both of us. I froze as the sound of scampering feet rushed down the steps. Tariq stood up in shock with his pants at his ankles, while my father now stood in the basement with us. Daddy reeked of liquor. Out of nowhere he grabbed a small pipe wrench and whacked Tariq in the head with it.

"The only niggers I'll have in this house goddamn it, are DEAD NIGGERS!" he slurred, before striking Tariq once more.

Tariq's head was split open. He fell backwards putting up a fight, but daddy grew stronger and restrained him very easily. I cried in fear as my father ripped off my panty hose. He tied Tariq's wrists to a cast iron pipe that spanned across the basement ceiling. Tariq was in a state of terror himself and could barely plead for my assistance. He just moaned in pain looking somewhat dazed.

I didn't know what my father was up to, but he had the same look in his eye as he did at the airport.

"NOOO! STOP!" Tariq shouted with the last bit of energy he had, as my father spread his butt cheeks apart.

By now I had stopped crying. I stared at my father in shock as he brutally raped a teenage boy in front of his daughter.

"Wanna' screw my little girl" he hollered with each stroke, "how does it feel with a dick up *YOUR* ass buddy! I lost everything because of you fucking niggers!"

"What are you doing daddy stop!" I cried out, "stop!"

My father just looked at me with a soulless stare, revealing the evil spirit that possessed his mind. I knew I should've helped Tariq, like call the police or something, but I couldn't find the strength to move. I was too petrified. Tariq's horrid screams continued and I think he even shit on himself cause I could smell a foul odor.

"I'll teach you both a lesson that you'll never forget," my father snapped in a sharp German accent, "you're just like your mother Patricia and you disobeyed me. I told you what I'd do if I ever caught you with one of these jungle bunnies...get over here!"

The taste of blood and shit almost made me puke and this was the first time I had a prick in my mouth that I didn't enjoy. In the most deranged manner my father rubbed his sperm into my skin as if it was Noxzema, then slapped me with his penis back and forth east to west.

Tariq cried silently as blood dripped from his torn anal canal down his leg.

"You made me do this" my father hollered out of breath, "you should've listened to me Patricia...now go to your room!"

I ran upstairs crying uncontrollably, with a hatred for my father that I thought I'd never have. When I got to my room I could hear Tariq getting beat to death while my father laughed like a maniac.

Scene Four:

We don't need no water let the muthafucka' burn

It felt like it took forever, but the day finally came for me to graduate. I was one step closer to living on my own. Seven miserable months had passed since that traumatic Halloween afternoon in the basement, and no matter how much time went by, everyday felt the same. I was an emotional mess. As it turned out, Tariq was very active in sports, so when he turned up missing posters went up everywhere. I even saw his face on a milk carton once.

I felt blameworthy about Tariq's callous death and to escape all the guilt built up inside, I got high everyday like Styles P. My drug habit skyrocketed faster than the price of gas. Cocaine was my new love, and any love I had in the past for my father was a vague memory. It was common for him to walk passed my bedroom door masturbating, while I did my homework. I was petrified of being in the house with him alone because he was fucking crazy for real for real.

To avoid further incestual encounters with my father, I started hanging in local clubs, where I stayed out all night long. Whoever I met at the club each night, would take me home with them. In a matter of months I ran through every nigga in the hood just to avoid coming home. That's how I think I caught crabs for the first time.

My nights were restless sleeping in a stranger's bed. Tariq's haunting screams replicated in my mind on a daily basis. I never told anyone what happened to Tariq and it was killing me to let someone know how I was feeling. If I told Tasha what I knew, she would beat my ass and call the police. I couldn't take it anymore. I had to tell somebody something or I was going to go nuts like my father.

I ran to my brother Chad, who showed me how much he really cared. Chad was fresh out of that DMT shit when I asked for some, so he gave me a shot of Thorazine instead. When I calmed down I told him exactly what happened and he flipped on me like it was my fault.

"Do you think I would turn my own father in over some nigger you fucked?" Chad shouted sounding offended, "If you stayed with your own kind none of this would've happened!"

Chad didn't give a shit about what my father did. He would have probably done the same thing. Chad was just as prejudiced as my father, and he just wanted to know if I had anal sex with a black man. When I was 10 years old Chad made me promise that I would never let anyone else penetrate me anally. He said it would be his special place and gift to him as his sister. I never counted my brother as being my first, so to me I was still a virgin until Ron hit it.

"Is my asshole the only thing you care about Chad?" I replied with much anger, "I thought I could come to you for comfort but you're just like daddy...fuck you man!"

"Well you obviously thought wrong sis," Chad retorted with a cynical comeback.

"Well *maybe* I should tell the police what you've been doing with dead people's body fluids and how you smuggle drugs back and forth to California or *maybe* I should tell your girlfriend about all the times you molested me growing up! How 'bout that?"

"You listen to me you little whore! I've been good to you all these years. You loved having sex with me so don't even try it. If you tell anyone about my thing in California I'll kill you myself," Chad gritted his teeth, "do you understand me!"

Chad was all talk and no action. He was a skinny punk that never won a fistfight in his life and I knew I could kick his ass if he took it further. When he grabbed my arm I backslapped him like a five-dollar trick on the 3rd before leaving his house.

As soon as I got back to New Haven I

walked to a liquor store two blocks from my house. I almost lost a track of time downing Heinekens and doing lines, and then went straight home to get ready for my high school graduation. It had started already at 5pm, so I didn't want to miss the whole thing. Being the big time tease that I was, I decided to only wear a bra and thong panties under my lightweight graduation gown.

I ended up arriving to the ceremony only minutes before my name was called. The last diploma was handed out and everyone threw their square caps in the air, screaming like a cowboys. We were all happy as hell.

"Fuck College, fuck my family, fuck everybody" were my exact sentiments if I recall correctly, *"I'm a grown ass woman now!"*

The only person that I did miss dearly was my mother. I wished she were there that day to share in my joy.

As I made my way outside all types of guys gave me hugs. They rubbed up against my body detecting that I was half naked under the thin rayon gown. Some niggas had the nerve to grab my ass like they knew me and of course the ones I slept with already asked me to go to their graduation parties. I declined each tempting offer and decided to keep it simple, even though I was hot and horny.

Instead of letting the fellas run a train on me this time, I just hung out on Dixwell Avenue with some girls from my homeroom. We got high and talked shit about all of our former classmates and teachers that we didn't like, then broke off for the night. While walking the long way home, I cringed as a billboard size poster of Tariq in his football uniform caught my attention. The peeling billboard attached to the side of a gas station read, "*If anyone has seen this person or has any information please call 1-800-missing.*"

My high was completely blown and for some reason I became enraged, breaking bottles and keying cars as I staggered home. When I finally reached the door it was almost 3 o'clock in the morning. I tried to creep inside through the back door, but it sounded like my father was still up arguing with somebody in the living room. My curiosity wouldn't let me go upstairs so I stayed in the kitchen to listen.

The next thing I heard was glass break then a lamp fell to the floor. I peeked my head around the kitchen corner to see who my father was talking to and oddly enough it was an old picture of my mother that he held a conversation with. The glass in the frame had shattered and being much more wasted than I was he didn't even realize that his hand was bleeding.

"*...Your purity was ruined, I had to cleanse your flaming soul. I saved you! I saved you! Leave me alone, stop haunting me or I'll kill your daughter too!*"

My heart dropped to a fetal position hesitant to function, as I overheard the truth about my mother's death. Daddy's drunken confession struck with such intensity that I couldn't move. As the vivid memory of my father ejaculating in my face flashed through my mind, so did every other demeaning incident in my life appear. Without explanation I placed a large Ginsu knife in my hand and pushed myself into the living room. I stood behind my father emotionless as I repeatedly drove the razor sharp blade into his back. I must have stabbed him over 33 times before I finally stopped.

All sounds muted as he fell face first crashing through the glass coffee table. I flipped my father around to look in his eyes, and then bent down to kiss him as if he were my lover. I sucked the last bit of breath from his lungs like he did to my virtue, then stood up and walked away. He was dead for sure and there was no way he was coming back.

For all these years I was under the impression that my mother had died from a rare lead poisoning disease, but that night I learned the truth. The lead poisoning she suffered was from the bullets my father fired into her chest when he caught her having sex with a black man. I felt like my mother's spirit used me to get revenge, and now she could rest in peace.

After doing a couple more lines of powder and fixing myself a sandwich, I dragged the heavy bastard into the basement. My impulsive plan was to cremate his body in the same fire chamber that Tariq burned in, but it was easier said than done. There was broken glass and a thick pool of blood on the carpet that would have been impossible to get out. Then another trail of blood all the way down to the basement.

"What the fuck am I gonna' do?" I thought, *"How can I make this look like an accident"* I wondered pacing back and forth.

That's when I came up with the idea to burn down the entire goddamn house. I fumbled through the boxes of embalming fluid stored in the basement then thought a little harder.

"I know, I'll make it look like he got drunk and started a fire while working with all these chemicals. Everyone knows daddy's a drunk and smokes cigars...maybe it'll work."

Before I set the blaze with one of my father's Cuban cigars, I rummaged through his wallet and removed all the cash he had, plus two bankcards, before putting it back in his pants pocket. As the smoke began to seep upstairs from the basement, I stuffed my mother's picture on top of the clothes I quickly packed, then got the hell out of there even faster. I waited in the backyard watching the house burn from a distance, before calling 911 from a neighbor's house. The last words out of my mouth concerning my piece of shit father were R.I.P.

"Rest-In-Piss motherfucker!"

The next day I sat in the police station blowing bubbles and popping chewing gum, while I waited in the station lobby. Chad was there and had already been questioned. Before Chad left the station he informed me that he was listed as the top beneficiary on daddy's life insurance policy and as soon as the check cleared, he'll give me my share if I kept my mouth shut about what I knew.

"Was Mr. Gubenhimer involved with any hate groups?" asked one cop, "Did Mr. Gubenhimer use or sell drugs?"

"At what time did you notice the house on fire?" his partner inquired.

This went on for about an hour. The investigators weren't charging me with Murder or Arson, they just wanted to question me about my father's business affairs. He was under investigation way before this. The detectives suspected that he was part of a white-collar ring that sold dead people's vital organs on the Internet and white market.

Needless to say I was familiar with the whole thing. I should've snitched on my brother to get him back for how he treated me days before, but I didn't.

"One last thing Patricia...were you planning a trip? Your neighbors stated that you had luggage or a bag with you when they answered the door?"

"I always walk around with a months supply of clothes" I answered then asked, "are we finished, I gotta' go?"

In a casual way the police warned me that the fire seemed suspicious before they let me go.

If my father's body didn't burn to ashes they might've had a case, but any idiot could see they were just grasping in the air for information.

For months I stayed at this rinky-dink motel until I could find a more stable place to live. My grandmother on my father's side lived in money earnin' MT. Vernon, NY and she offered her extra bedroom to me, if I wanted to stay there, but I declined. My other Grandma, the nosey wrinkled rich one in California, wanted me to live with her, but when it came time to board the plane I conveniently missed the flight.

In three weeks I withdrew over $5000 using my father's debit cards at ATM machines. It was just about all he had following the lawsuit, but I made do. Nobody was going to stop me from doing things my way. This was my chance to be grown and live on my own. I figured if things didn't work out with my little ghetto adventure, then I'll just move out to California with Jenny.

Scene Five:

Duane Reade

A year had passed since I offed my pops and I hadn't shed a tear over his ass once. It was a typical Thursday morning in May and like any other time after my weekly Brazilian bikini wax, I hit Chiffon's House of Glamour and Gossip, the flyest beauty salon in the New Haven area. The salon was unusually packed this particular day. High school girls were piling in to get dolled up for the prom, so it was a busy mess.

My brows needed trimming and my nails were starting to look a little roach too, but the real reason why I frequented the place so much was for the latest scoop. I learned things like who did who, who made the most money doing what in the streets, who was gay and best of all, who had the biggest dick in the hood. For a white girl like me who wasted hours watching rap videos to pick up style and slang, hanging out in Chiffon's was a 101 course in street savoir-faire. It was certainly the bomb spot to parlay in if you wanted to get known in the streets. Every woman in there was a ghetto superstar, especially the beauticians. At this point I considered myself a star, since I spent a fortune on stylish clothes and hung out with the beauty shop's owner.

As I walked through the door in a pair of tight Baby Phat jeans and a skimpy *Got Dick?* logo T-shirt, the door chime sounded. Everyone paused to check out the new shiny bracelets on my arm before carrying on with their conversations. I received all types of jealous stares. My shit was bling blingin'! I knew them chicks in there were jelly, because they all rolled their eyes in disgust. I rolled my eyes right back at 'em before sitting down to get my refill.

"Girl...as long as I'm gettin' my pussy licked in the tropics I don't care how he makes his money" laughed one of the sassy beauticians, "how many niggas around here take you to St. Lucia just to get some ass?"

"Aren't you scared of gettin' arrested or even shot, messin' wit' dat' wild nigga?" a customer interjected, before her head was placed into the rinse sink.

"I ain't never scared!" Rita declared.

"I don't know about your man Rita, but Duane knows not to mix his business with my pleasure. I'm a pro, not a hoe," Chiffon answered with a feminine three snaps up, three snaps down, "you bitches need to read more learn more and change the globe wit' 'dat pussy."

Chiffon Davis ran the place and out of all of the women in there she was the most restrained. I mean she could gossip with the best of them, but she was more laid back. Chiffon was that sexy conceited chick all the hustlers tried to get with. She had a body that wouldn't quit with an attitude to go with it. Most dudes were too scared to approach Chiffon because she was that beautiful. They figured what was the point in trying to get with someone who they know would only turn them down.

At one time I was involved with Chiffon's younger brother Breeze. Even though things didn't work out between Breeze and I, Chiffon never held a grudge against me and we stayed mad cool with each other. She taught me how to attack a nigga's mind game. Chiffon said tackle his strengths, rather than go after his weaknesses. If the guy looks good, make him feel like he's ugly. If he has a big dick, let him know that you had bigger. Even if you really haven't, she said, lie about it, cause in doing so he'll feel like he has something to prove and you'll always have the upper hand.

Chiffon was like my personal street advisor and I was so jealous of her it wasn't even funny. Not of her looks and street smarts, but jealous of whom she was engaged to. I always acted totally naïve around Chiffon and I let her believe what she wanted to believe to get closer. I think she thought I was this dumb white girl with big titties who needed schooling. I guess that's why she took me under her wing.

"So tell me" Sandy the nail technician asked a girl sitting next to me as she did my nails, "how did things go with you and my lil' cousin yesterday?"

"I should kick you in your damn mouth! That nigga had too many nots" the girl replied, "...not big enough, not hard enough and not paid enough and his breath smelled like shit on top of that!"

"Sandy? What did I tell you about that hook up bullshit" Chiffon placed her hands on her hips as she stopped weaving a client's hair, "you really need to quit. How many times are you gonna' try to set somebody up with those cornball cousins of yours? You're giving my business a bad name sweetie, come on get it together gurl."

"I remember when Sandy tried to hook me up with her brother" a customer out of nowhere uttered, "I come outside to meet the man right, and this silly ass nigga is wearin' headphones holding a bouquet of sky blue plastic roses! His car looked like it had cancer and the engine was all smokin' and shit. I ran back in the house and locked my damn door!"

While silly laughter broke out inside the shop, the large storefront windows which proudly broadcast the name "Chiffon's House of Glamour and Gossip" in big audacious gold letters, began to vibrate from the pounding base sounds of Smooth the Hustler and Trigga' the gambler's rap classic, Broken Language.

"...*The Glock cocker-The block locker- The rock chopper-The shot popper... The human drug generator-The honey gamer The chicken tricka'-The slicka' long dick pussy sticka'-The ready to bust that ass kicka'...*" blasted outside of Chiffon's salon, as a one of a kind custom made cherry drop top Range Rover pulled to the curb and parked.

Chiffon fixed her apron then threw a mint in her mouth for freshness. The entire salon grew quiet. The sexiest thug of the year hopped out draped in jewels. His broad shoulders filled out the crisp Banana Republic dress shirt that he wore and his jeans didn't hang off his ass like the jeans of his workers. In spite of this, the heap of platinum chains and medallions around his neck overshadowed Duane's clean-cut appearance.

Duane was blazin and he knew it. He walked through the door like he owned the place, because basically he did. Ironically Duane's last name was Read and like *Duane Reade*, the popular chain of pharmacy stores in New York City, this Duane Read sold just as much drugs, maybe more.

"Sup' ladies" the chocolate heartthrob greeted everyone, "where'd my suga' booga' disappear to that quick?"

Duane was referring to Chiffon who had

stepped in the back to get more hair.

"What did I tell you about blasting your music 'round here" Chiffon complained as she re-entered the room, "this is a respectable business baby and all that loud music shit is tacky."

Rather than jump into his arms and give the man a dynamic tongue kiss like anyone else would have done, Chiffon treated Duane indifferent with complaints. She even pushed his hand away when he attempted to pinch her ass.

"Stop playin' yo and give me a kiss," Duane chuckled as he pulled his woman close, "I got something for you."

Chiffon opened the Littman jewelers bag then kissed Duane on the cheek. She tried on the diamond earrings in front of all the customers who just oooed and ahhed.

While the chatty employees and customers stayed in Duane's mouth listening to every word, I got up out my chair. Outside in the passenger seat sat one of Duane's lieutenants. He waved me out to the truck to talk, but I pointed at myself acting like I didn't know which girl he was referring to.

"Who Me?" I spoke silently through the window.

Buck kept shaking his head yes as I continued to point.

"Why don't you just go outside and see what he wants?" Duane said in his deep raspy voice, "I think he wants to get with you."

"If Buck had any class he would come in here to talk for himself" Chiffon intervened, "and since when did you become Cupid Duane?"

"Its okay girl, as long as he's not related to Sandy" I shared a smile with Duane, "it's all good right!"

Sandy smacked her lips in repugnance as I switched my ass to the exit to meet Duane's friend. I leaned over the passenger side door to make it look like I was really interested in Buck, but I really wanted Duane to get a good view of my booty poking out. Chiffon taught me that a girl could never go wrong in tight jeans and heels and she was right. I don't care if a man is with his wife or not, if you walk sexy in high heels and tight jeans he will find someway to check you out no matter what.

"How long do you think you can keep this shit up?" Buck huffed at me.

"As long as we can" I shot back.

"I'm gettin' tired of this bullshit yo! My girl thinks I'm cheatin' on her ass cause of y'all" Buck snapped again, "If Duane is so big and bad why don't he just come clean and let Chiffon know what time it is!"

"What do you know about game... you're just a small soldier so play your position. Chiffon don't have a clue about me and Duane, so let her high and mighty ass think she's number one" I laughed, "now smile cause everyone's looking at us."

To make it look good I let Buck slap my ass

before I walked back in the salon. From inside the shop it appeared like Buck was the man and I was laughing at his charming conversation, but the whole thing was a sham. I had been fucking Duane for months already. Matter of fact, Duane was the one who gave me the $3000 bangle bracelets on my arm that Chiffon complimented me on when I first walked in.

"Oh my god I didn't know Buck was so cute" I said as I sat back down in my chair, "he wants to take me out to eat...should I go with them?" I asked Chiffon.

"Them Who? There's more than one?" Chiffon responded suspiciously.

"No I mean him, should I go with Buck to lunch was what I meant to say?"

"You told me you didn't like niggas with dread locks, now all of a sudden you think Buck's cute?"

I just shrugged my shoulders before Duane cut in.

"Bay, I hope you like your earrings. I gotta' go out'a town for a minute so I'll see ya' tonight okay?" Duane kissed Chiffon on the forehead, "call me if you need anything."

"Where exactly out of town are you going?" Chiffon promptly inquired.

"Um...what's it called?" Duane pondered like a fool, "um?"

"Milford..." I accidentally uttered, then covered myself by saying, "Oh your boy just mentioned something about going to Milford, is that where you're talking about?"

Chiffon gave us a strange look, because a lie lingered in the air and the truth could be smelled from a distance. If she stared at Duane any harder his eyes would have confessed everything.

"How in the hell does she know where *my* man is goin' before I do!" Chiffon pulled Duane to the side, "what's goin' on baby, you're actin' funny?"

"Nothin' baby I gotta' go, I'll see you tonight."

As I hopped in the back of DR's Rover to supposedly get dropped off with Buck, I waved bye to Chiffon, but she didn't look too happy about me riding in the back of her man's truck without her in the front. Chiffon used to joke all the time on how her man was lactose intolerant, meaning that he couldn't stand white girls, but as soon as Duane met me he came down with a little jungle fever.

...Duane and I first met when I was staying at the Branford Inn, a motel outside of New Haven. We literally met by accident. I was driving Chiffon's brother Breeze's rental down Dixwell avenue one day, trying to roll a blunt and drive at the same time, then slammed into the back of Duane's Beemer. He jumped out ready to kick my ass until noticing that I was a female, a fly one I might add.

Duane's nostrils flared as he bit down on his lip checking me out. He had that *I'd love to get me some of that* look in his eye, so I stepped out the car to let him feast his eyes on the rest of me. Duane moved back to let me out, licking his lips the whole time.

"Yo you okay?" He eventually asked.

"I should be asking you that question," I batted my eyes, "I'm sorry, I wasn't paying attention."

Duane didn't know that I knew Chiffon at the time, so he kept staring at my shear top, which exposed my huge pink areolas. My nipples were so hard they could have cut glass.

"Well it doesn't look that bad" I stated while bending over to look at the damage.

Given that I didn't have any panties on under my short skirt, I knew Duane was peeking and getting aroused.

"*It doesn't look that bad?*" Duane scowled, "look at my shit! Those used to be custom LED tail lights now look at 'em!"

I got scared for a minute cause I thought he was going to report the accident. Breeze would have had a fit, especially since I didn't have my license yet.

"Don't worry about it" Duane said, "You're lucky you're cute. I'll have one of my mechanics fix it, but you should watch where you're goin' next time."

I knew Duane had long money, so I thought to myself, "*fuck Chiffon, this is my chance to bag a big time nigga...go for it bitch.*"

I gave a seductive smile as I walked circles

around Duane in a flirtatious kind of way and said, "Well since I hit you from the back I guess... I should return the favor and let you hit me from the back."

When I poked out my ass Duane became tantalized.

"Do you think you can you handle it?" I whispered in his ear as I slowly traced my protruding nipples with my fingernail.

I caught him off guard, so it took Duane a minute to respond.

"Shiiit..." he shifted his crotch, "you might get whiplash fuckin' wit' me nah'mean?"

"Well guess what? I like it ruff big boy" I said as I tossed him my room key, "and if you can beat me to the telly you can give me whiplash, dicklash, or whatever else you wanna' beat me with."

Duane ran back to his car thrilled as hell. The challenge excited him even more. He floored it into a u-turn, while I was already passed the light headed for the entrance ramp. It was like we were in a cannonball run and sex was the prize. Breeze's Pontiac Rental car that I drove was no match for the 745I BMW that Duane drove, so of course he won.

"What took you so long?" Duane laughed when I finally entered the room, "I got forty-five minutes so face down and ass up!"

Duane's assertive manner made me hotter than a bowl of southern grits. He sucked my nipples through my thin shirt then stripped me down until I was ass naked.

"Wait a minute?" I complained on all fours acting as if I was a little schoolgirl, "can I please have a piece of candy first mister?"

"Sure...do you like Mr. Good Bars," Duane played along, "it melts in your mouth not in your hand.

"Oh my gawd!" I laughed in astonishment, "That thing's enormous!"

Duane stuffed the entire length of his monster down my throat and I didn't even gag. Over the years my mouth had become a regular sperm receptacle and he didn't know that I could drink a man better than Jenna Jameson. Duane loved it when I tried to talk while swallowing his huge cock, and take it from me, etiquette is not a factor when you're sucking dick.

The dirtier I talked the more turned on Duane became, trembling with ecstasy. I knew in twenty minutes after the award winning blowjob I preformed, Duane would be eating out of the palm of my hand or should I say, the crack of my ass. He ordered me to stop then placed my legs behind my head like a yogi.

It was as if my vagina was the Matrix as Duane went in and out in a slow motion manner switching his deep energetic strokes to hyper speed thrusts. Duane's long shaft and bulbous head felt like a meat missile exploding inside of me as he let out a manly moan.

"Aawwwww!" He sounded as he came all over my back.

"Aw'man you shoulda' told me you were cummin'" I pouted, "I wanted to do my thing."

Duane looked at his chrome Tag Heuer watch then gasped with a relieving grin, "fifteen more minutes can't hurt, let me see what I can do" he said, as he left handedly stroked his penis.

I wasn't into any R. Kelly type shit, but I liked to be splashed in the face with spunk. Hot sperm made my skin clear. My sister Jenny used baby urine on her face, I'd rather have a cum facial on mine, but to each their own.

"Stop being silly" I laughed at how fast Duane jerked himself off, "I got you baby just lay back and let me work it."

First I massaged Duane all over his body to get the nerve endings circulating again, and then I worked the middle with my long pierced tongue. In no time Duane's third leg was revived. After some more deep anal sex, I gave Duane the tug job of his life, until he gushed a happy ending all over my grill. Satisfaction guaranteed.

Following our first episode at the motel, I could've planted a flag on Duane's behind, cause that ass was mine now. He testified that I was the nastiest chick he had ever been with. Chiffon never took it in the face and by no means was she going to suck him off in between a nasty butt fucking. She was wifey, but I was Duane's very own porno star.

Scene Six:
Something better at home

When Duane found out how close Chiffon and I were, he started giving me all types of expensive gifts to keep me quiet. I could not afford to stay at a motel any longer and given the fact that Duane had big chips, I convinced him to move me into an apartment on Edgewood Avenue. Duane paid for the first two months rent and security deposit, but said I would have to pay my own rent from then on. He trusted me enough to stash some of his drugs in my apartment, which was all good with me, because I sniffed a little here and there whenever I wanted to. He had no idea that I was the type of bitch to backstab you when you least expected it.

After weeks of intensive scrutinizing, I finally discovered Duane's weakness and it wasn't great head and good pussy. D-R was poor growing up, so now that he was paid, he wanted more than nothing to be accepted by white people as a successful black man. Rather than emulate their own rich and noble heritage, niggas like this imitate other races and think that in order to be truly successful, he has to have a White girl trophy on his arm.

Instead of the usual routine of hanging out in the hood, Duane often hit the suburbs to flaunt me around. I think he got off on the reaction people gave us when we walked down the street arm and arm. I introduced Duane to all of my uppity friends from Wallingford and they eventually set up a nice little drug trade on the college campus circuit for us. Most of their parents were political or prominent members of the community and in a few short months, Duane and I were "the couple" to invite to your party if you needed narcotic catering.

Meeting my friends is what really blew Duane's business up. It gave him the opportunity to expand his operation all over Connecticut and lock up the market. Before getting involved with me, Duane had most of his money invested in coke and crack, which was very profitable on its own. When I showed him how much new money there was in designer drugs, he invested heavily in them too. We set up stash houses in every dorm on every college campus in the area. Duane hired workers that looked like Mork and Mindy and even had security guards moving product for him.

Seeing as Duane was making so much money off of my ideas, I thought he would hit me off with stacks of doe, but he was tight when it came to giving up cash. Yeah he bought me a $10,000 Chinchilla fur and a few designer dresses, but I felt like saying *fuck all these gifts and hand over the money instead!*

In this game I learned that in order to stay on top you need to be needed, so I made sure that I remained the middle man between Duane and my friends or I was gonna' be wearing rabbit fur soon. I started my own little thing on the side, lacing already good weed with embalming fluid to enhance its potency. In addition to that I made Rophnol and Ecstasy suppositories for the Rave parties. In this form, X lasted 2 to 3 hours longer. Club kids didn't have to worry anymore about getting caught with drugs in their pockets, when they could easily stick a suppository up their ass to get high while they danced.

If I had to estimate how much money I brought in for Duane compared to myself, it would easily be in the quarter to half a mill range. I deserved way more money than the small allowance Duane gave me for all the shit I stored and carried for him, but fuck it I enjoyed being his bitch at the time.

The day Duane and Buck picked me up from Chiffon's salon, he took me to my spot to re-up on some product before heading down to

Milford. Unfortunately there was someone waiting for us that I did not want to see.

"What does he want now?" I sighed, when noticing Manny's car parked in front of my apartment.

In or out of prison, Manny was still a fucking pest. On his second furlough he tracked me down for some pussy and I regretfully broke him off a little piece. Two weeks after we had sex, I told Manny I was pregnant by him and needed money for an abortion. His gullible ass believed it, and gave me $400 that I think I used on a pair of shoes to wear to the club.

The only good thing I liked about Manny was that he was a total thug. Some chicks might not admit it, but every woman keeps a crazy nigga in their pocket for those times when they need beef settled or whatever. Other than that, Manny was worthless. He was terrible in bed and drove a throwback Maxima that everyone else called a hooptie. I kept Manny around as my run to guy, until I met Duane and witnessed how feared he was in the streets.

As we pulled to the curb I caught sight of the slightly jealous look on Duane's face, so I kissed him on the lips and told him what the deal between Manny and I was when he asked, "Is that your little boyfriend?"

"Hell no! He's just some nobody I used to fuck wit' a long time ago" I said, "He won't leave me alone that's all."

"If this kid got a problem we can handle it

right now," Duane said as he reached for his gun.

"Chill baby... that's not necessary I'll be right back."

I hopped out Duane's Rover before he parked. Manny mean mugged Duane while he tried figuring out who he was when I opened the door.

"Where da' hell you been at?" Manny yelled out, "I've been waitin' out here for an hour already! I told you I was comin' by to get my shit!"

"What shit? That beat up Yankee cap and ODB CD!" I hollered back just as loud, "that's the only things you ever left in my crib so stop lying!"

Manny called me all kinds of bitches and hoes then flicked his blunt at Duane's windshield. I rushed up the steps struggling with his tight grip on my arm, until Duane jumped out of his truck to pull us apart.

"Mende go upstairs and stop arguing wit' his ass," Duane instructed as Manny released his grip.

Duane was not as muscular as Manny, but he was still strong and in excellent shape.

"Yo get the fuck off me son and mind ya' fuckin' business before you get hurt!" Manny lashed out like he was the hardest thing since Tony Montana, "Dis' between me and my girl homie! Who da' fuck you think you is anyway?

"I suggest you bounce before you find out!"

Duane said before pushing Manny to the ground, "Mende is my business!"

As soon as I came back outside Manny tried to act hard in front of me. He got up off the ground and rushed Duane like a football player. Unflustered with the athletic moves of a running back, Duane easily dodged the tackle. He then displayed a .357 Magnum, which stopped Manny dead in his tracks. Manny threw up some gang sign as he backed away on all fours.

"We ain't in jail fool," Duane laughed as he mocked Manny by throwing up K.S.I and the Hill gang signs.

Manny's face filled with trepidation as Duane stood over him with the Magnum. He pistol-whipped Manny across the face three times, leaving him bloody and bruised on the cement walkway.

"And don't let me catch you 'round here no more son! You understand!"

"I'ight chill man don't shoot!" Manny pleaded with dirty grass and blood falling from his mouth, "please man don't do it!"

"Baby that's enough let's go," I laughed at how stupid Manny looked crawling away.

For some reason violence excited me. I got off on the shit. Only in the hood could I experience such a thrill of two niggas fighting over me.

"I'm glad you didn't blast him in front of my neighbors" I exhaled as we drove away, "the last thing I need is police asking me questions and shit."

"I'm glad you already know that" Duane looked me in the face, "from now on I don't want anybody at your crib except me you got that?"

"But what happens if Manny tries to come back at me for what you did to him. What should I do then?"

"Trust me, son don't want nothin'...I'm 'dat nigga you don't wanna' fuck wit' Na'mean...*Call me Mister what's really good, I'm so hood, niggas know not to fuck wit D-R, I'm up to no good, packin' chrome burners for slow learners, I got all types of tools for fools wit' silly problems, two shots from the three fifty seven easily solves 'em...*"

Although I giggled at Duane's little rhyme, I didn't feel as confident as he did. I knew Manny would seek retribution.

While Duane continued to spit his cocky rhyming skills, I flexed a blunt to take my mind off of everything and threw in Manny's ODB CD I decided to keep. Fifteen minutes later we pulled into the Connecticut Post Mall and parked.

"Take this to Footlocker" Duane said, "there'll be a tall brother named Romell at the counter and give him the code before handing over the bag."

"You went through all that bullshit with Chiffon just to have me deliver a fucking package?" I exhaled the weed smoke in his face, "what's the damn code?"

"Just say *I need a cash refund...the receipt's in the bag.*"

"We gotta' talk when I get back."

"About what?" Duane wondered as I passed him the Dutch.

"About us what'chu think."

The transaction went smoothly and I was in and out of the mall in two minutes. When I returned I thought I'd mentioned to Duane that as a business associate and fuck buddy I deserved more. If I was supposed to be Duane's Bonnie in this thing like he said, then why did I feel like I was being used?

See at first I was merely in search of a paid nigga with a platinum dick, but now I was starting to catch feelings for this cat. It wasn't so much about the money, as it was about where I stood compared to Chiffon.

"This shit ain't working out Duane I need more!"

"More what...money?" He said

"You know what I'm talkin' about nigga don't play dumb, I need more out of our entire relationship. You don't seem to have a problem parading me around the suburbs, but when we're in the hood you act like you're scared to be seen with me, what's up?"

"Here we go" Duane sighed, "you must've been watchin' Oprah again or some shit Dr. Phil co-signed."

"No fuck that! I'm tired of watching Chiffon treat you like a child. She's your ghetto princess and I'm your suburb mistress. All she does is spend your money. I don't even know why you're still with her stuck up ass?"

"Hold up Mende, I make the money and you get the dick that's basically it. Chiffon's a real money earner not to mention my son's mother, so she could spend doe all damn day if she wants to, cause that's what wifey does."

"I'm not a fuckin' money earner!" I shouted in outrage before throwing the three-inch thick knot of cash that the footlocker dude gave me, "all I did was introduce you to cash! Fuck this shit! From now on do your own transactions!"

"What'chu want me to do Mende, break up with Chiffon and make you my number one cause you introduced me to a few college kids?" Duane laughed, like the thought was absurd, "You got a fat ass and all that baby, but I ain't leaving Chiffon for no white chick from out the mountains! You crazy?"

Duane flipped through the money like a deck of cards then tried to hand it back like it was mine.

"Fine. If you don't want it, I'll give the money to someone else" he said after I pushed his hand away.

"You think I'm some bird bitch don't you?" I retorted, "My family is fucking rich I don't need you or your fucking money Duane! Just take me home I'm through with you."

Oh my god I was fuming at what Duane said. I didn't say a word for the entire ride back to New Haven now that I knew how he truly felt about me. This bastard tried to play me like I was Teena Marie and he was Rick James. I almost slipped and called him the black ass nigger that he was, but I caught myself. Losing me didn't only mean losing some good ass, it also meant losing a lot of customers. So after Duane thought about it more, he began kissing my ass.

"You still mad," Duane tapped me to break the silence, "you look cute when you're mad, you know that?"

Duane made sexy eyes at me then said, "I can't leave Chiffon that easily. You don't understand... it's deeper than our son."

He started rubbing my breast and feeling my leg while he drove. All Duane had to do was touch me and I forgot how mad I was. It was like he never said what he did.

"Who lives here?" I asked when we pulled up to this posh, although modest home on Whitney Avenue, "cause I'm not running no more packages for you."

"Does this really look like a crack house?" Duane laughed.

The house was small enough to keep the FEDS away, but the row of luxury vehicles parked in the drive way let you know what time it was. I could have melted in the seat when Duane told me it was his crib. Like a ten year old walking into Disney World I smiled ear to ear as we pulled into the garage.

"You said never let nobody know where you rest your head, why you bringing me here now?" I questioned.

"Cause I felt like it" Duane affirmed, "Chiffon don't wear the pants I'm the fuckin' boss!"

According to Duane I was the first chick that he ever brought to his home outside of his fiancé. He said that I should feel honored, because he would probably never do it again. I guess this was his way of making up for how he treated me earlier.

Duane carried me up to the bedroom as someone else in the house played 50 Cent's P.I.M.P song.

"I don't know what you heard about me... but white pussy is the B-O-M-B! G-G-G-G-UNIT!"

"We need to get you a record deal" Duane sarcastically commented as I sang along, "jump in the shower and I'll be back in a minute."

While Duane ran downstairs to get the phone, I curiously checked out every room upstairs. At the same time as Chiffon gossiped at her salon about other girl's men who were creeping, I was in miss bad ass' bedroom standing stark naked skimming through her jewelry box. Before I got in the shower I called the salon on my cell to make sure Chiffon was still there and not on her way home.

"Chiffon's glamour and gossip, Tina speaking..."

"Hi is Chiffon there?"

"Chiffon's with a client right now can I take a message?"

"No that's okay, I was just wondering if she had time to fit me in for a wash and set today?"

"Girl Chiffon's gonna' have her hands full for at least 4 more hours, do you want me to..."

All I needed to hear was 4 hours, and then I hung up in Tina's face. That was more than enough time for Duane and I to stain the sheets with each other's orgasm juice. It was time to freshen up.

"Who the hell are you!" I screamed in shock as the shower door unexpectedly slid open with a stranger standing there.

"I'm Duane's lil' brother Terrell" he voiced, while gawking at my lathered body.

"Duane!" I persistently called out, "yo Duane!"

"Chill...D-R had to step out for a minute," Terrell gladly informed me, "when you got out the shower he told me to tell you that he'd be back in twenty minutes."

"Obviously you don't listen!" I snapped, "but when I was your age I liked to see naked bodies too...do you like what you see Terrell?"

Terrell just shook his head yes, while grinning ear to ear as he looked me up and down.

"Good, now close the door."

Terrell was aroused from what he saw, because his sweat pants grew in the front and that horny smile said it all. He was cute for his age and on any other day I would have pulled him in the shower with me and rode his skinny ass like a witch on a broomstick. But I figured, why chase a sip of fine wine when you can drink the whole bottle.

After rinsing off I paraded around the bedroom in one of Chiffon's terry cloth robes. I laid out on her king-sized bed then lightly sprayed the satin sheets with a mist of my own perfume. Chiffon was going to go crazy when she found the strands of blonde hair I left on the pillow. She told me once that she thought her assistant had the hots for Duane, so I wrote Tina's cell number on a piece of paper and slid it under the jewelry box to fuck with her head.

The next deceitful thing I did hoping to stir up a little conflict, was smear a smidgen of lipstick on the fly of Duane's jeans that were balled up in the hamper. Lastly I tossed my draws under the bed and laughed. When I heard Duane pull into the garage, I hurried downstairs like I just got out the shower.

"I swear yo, I can't stand Chiffon's pops! He thinks I'm his slave or some shit" I overheard Duane say with a belligerent attitude, "he called me over his house just to move a goddamn couch! Can you believe that shit Rell?"

It all started making sense to me why Duane kissed Chiffon's butt so much. Her father was a prominent Judge. Choosing to stay with her over me had nothing to do with beauty at all. Chiffon was his get outta' jail free bitch. Her father knew exactly what Duane did for a living, but was not going to let his grandson grow up with a daddy behind bars. Judge Davis kept Duane's drug dealing ass out of prison all these years, because his little girl fell in love a hustler.

"Yo Rell take this up to my bedroom then go play some video games" Duane instructed Terrell when I strolled into the kitchen. Duane undid my robe and offhandedly whispered, "Get on your knees."

I was his whore and he knew it. Anally and orally. Whatever hole he wanted to use it didn't matter. We fucked right there on the cold marble kitchen floor then did it again in the master bathroom. Two grams and a couple of snorts later, Duane filled the tub up with the case of Cristal that he made Terrell carry up from the pantry. Whenever Duane was fed up with Chiffon or her family he would always get drunk or carelessly waste money.

"Wouldn't this be fun if we could do this everyday" I stated as Duane pulled on his cig, "$3000 Champaign baths and a nice long hard fuck on the daily can make a woman do crazy things. Chiffon better watch her back," I playfully threatened.

"That's how I feel about her father" Duane sounded stressed, "I hope that muthafucka' has a heart attack the next time he decides to move some furniture."

"I'm here for you baby" I spoke softly as I massaged Duane's tense shoulders, "forget about Chiffon and her father" I sucked my teeth, "she's a gimmick anyway, I'm the real deal and you know I'll do anything for you... you want me to kill 'em?"

"Stop buggin'" Duane frowned, "I ain't saying all that."

Duane ended up drinking an entire bottle of Cristal by himself. He let his guard down and started talking about how much money he had stashed and what he planned to do with it and all that. He didn't have to prove nothing to me, but his ego wouldn't let him stop bragging. I finally caught him slipping.

Duane even made a drunken promise to take me to the Funk Master Flex auto show in Hartford, that I was going to hold him to when he sobered up the next day if he fronted.

"But Chiffon told me that you were taking your son to the UniverSoul Circus that weekend? How you gonna' pull this one off?" I wondered.

"If I say we're goin' to the car show goddamn it! Then that's where we're goin I said!"

While Duane went on and on about how much he hated Chiffon's father, I tuned him out and selfishly thought about myself and what I was going to wear. For the next five days our routine consisted of sniffing eight's, counting drug money and screwing in public places. I made sure Duane came at least three times, before I sent him home each night.

The Auto Show weekend ultimately came

and I couldn't wait to go. All of the big dogs were going to be there, so I had to look hot. At the last minute I decided to strut my stuff in a $7000 silk Gucci cocktail dress that I bought in Beverly Hills, instead of wearing the run of the mill Dolce & Gabbana outfit that I borrowed from Chiffon's closet.

I can't begin to tell you how spicy I looked. The way that smooth silk clung to my curves made it obvious that I was wearing nothing underneath. My ass shook like Jell-O hello! Oh and my shoe game was sick. Free from *106 & Park* had nothing on me. I had more boots than the Army, Navy, Air Force and Marines put together, but nobody could mess with the $2000 Australian gator knee high FMB (short for Fuck Me Boots) I wore that day.

Since Chiffon's Jewelry box was just sitting in the bedroom collecting dust, I assumed that she wouldn't miss any of it. Her diamond choker looked splendid on me I must say. Duane bought Chiffon and I so much jewelry that he didn't even notice I was wearing his fiancé's necklace.

When we got to the Civic Center it was off the chain. Duane left all the ghetto fabulous rides parked at home and more suitably drove us in his Canary yellow Bentley. The entire place was wall to wall packed with certified hustlers and auto lovers alike.

We must have snapped pictures with like every rap star in the building. Though most of the rappers had wives or model looking chicks by their side, niggas still kept their eyes on yours truly and they weren't looking at my boots! Even the hardcore pro-black MC's tried to holla' at me on the low. Just like car owners exhibited shiny exotic vehicles, I displayed the new phenomenon of white girls with exotic booty. Duane never held his arm around my waist as much as he did that day. You couldn't tell me nothing, except *you go girl!*

Scene Seven:

Critical Beat down

After the star-studded event, we got something to eat at Belly's Take-Out in Hartford. It was my idea to pick up some fast food, because I couldn't wait to show Duane a good time for showing me a good time. He wanted to get a room at the Branford Inn for old times sake, but I pleaded that he take me to his house again for other reasons. I massaged his balls for most of the ride home, but never touched his massive hard-on not even once. I made Duane starve for my wetness as if he never hit it before. He practically begged me for head, but I wouldn't do that either.

I teased Duane so much that his mushroom looking dickhead turned purple. It throbbed uncontrollably and I couldn't wait to unleash its tension. So as soon as we pulled up to the crib it was on! The fact that I wasn't wearing any panties made it easy for Duane to lick me as I bent over the hood of his Bentley. Duane sipped and blew on my sensitive clitoris like a person drinking hot coco before he dug me out. He flipped me around then wrapped my hair around his hand as he pulled my head back like I was a horse and he was the jockey in charge.

Oh my god I'll never forget how good it felt to feel the heat from the car's engine against my back when Duane switched positions to slam it porno style. I experienced waves of orgasmic sensations that only Duane could give. The garage door wasn't even closed yet and this nigga had my knees pressed to my chest fucking me like an epileptic on speed. If the neighbors across the street were watching us, they got to see one hell of a show.

Only seconds after the hardest orgasm I had ever felt in my life dripped down my inner-thigh, my entire mood plummeted faster than Martha Stewarts ImClone stock.

"Oh shit!" I yelled out, "stop Duane, stop!"

Duane thought stop meant, *keep going I want more*, but this time I really meant stop.

"I CAN'T BELIEVE THIS SHIT!" yelled Chiffon as she stormed up the driveway with a clear view of Duane still inside of me, "OH HELL NO!" She said.

"Oh my god Chiffon!" was Duane's first response, "It's a mistake baby let me explain!"

"Yeah right you tripped and slipped in her pussy by accident you lyin' bastard" Chiffon screamed, "How could you do this to me!

...*WHAP!*"

She smacked Duane in the head with the mini Yankee bat in her hand. Chiffon's cousin Kim rushed the boys back into the Range Rover as Chiffon chased me around Duane's Escalade in a livid rage.

"Breeze was right" Chiffon spat as I blocked her wild bat swings, "you ain't nothin' but a triflin' whore Mende! ...*WHAP!*"

The next thing I know I was on the ground. Chiffon kept kicking and kicking, as I laid there curled up in a ball. Given that I didn't really know how to rumble yet, I didn't fight back and could only defend myself. The blows to my head ultimately knocked me unconscious.

"Oh no she's not!" Chiffon uttered in disbelief, "I know this white trash bitch ain't wearing my fuckin' birthday present Kim!"

Chiffon snatched her jewelry off my neck then started crying in anger as if she was grief-stricken. She also took my Prada bag, which contained all of the money I had to my name. She thought it was hers too, but it wasn't. Duane had just bought us the same exact one like he always did with everything.

Eventually Chiffon stopped jabbing me in the stomach. She was totally heartbroken and her anger seemed to turn into sadness.

"I hate you D-R how could you!" Chiffon voiced out the window as she pulled off in an emotional fury, "it's over mutha'fucka' you hear me!"

While I crawled from up under the truck thinking the worst was over, I had another thing coming. Duane outrageously continued to beat my ass where Chiffon left off. He said it was my fault that his forthcoming marriage was ruined, like I put a gun to his head and made him screw me.

"I love you Duane!" I wept at his feet like a two year old begging him to stop, "Why are you doing this to me!" I cried, "Please Duane I love you!"

"Shut up bitch! I knew..." Duane paused his declaration as he began to slap me around, "we should've...*Pow!*" he punched me in the head, "...went to a hotel...*Bam!*...like I said...*Boom!* White bitches like you ain't nothin' but trouble...*Bam!*"

The last punch knocked me out. Duane then picked me up to carry my limp body over to the pile of foul-smelling garbage bags on the curb. He tossed me in it before jumping in his car to catch up to Chiffon.

By now I felt like a piece of trash. In no way did I ever expect Duane to do me like this. Here I was beat up and busted with my ass hanging out of my torn Gucci dress and a shiner under my left eye, walking down Whitney Avenue half barefoot with one broken boot heel. My lip was split and handfuls of hair were ripped out of my head, so I looked like I had survived a plane crash.

When I finally got home I collapsed on the

couch in a dejected frame of mind. My sense of worth was destroyed once again and to make matters worse I accidentally stepped in a large pile of dog shit that was hidden in the grass walkway near my building. My entire body was in complete agony. I just wanted to go to sleep and dream myself away.

The next morning I awoke to the thumping sounds of my fed up landlord demanding that I open the door and give him his money. To his apprehension I changed the locks, so he couldn't get in or confiscate my things like he did to the other tenants that didn't pay rent. I just stared at myself in the mirror in a sort of trance like state, ignoring his countless legal threats. I couldn't pay him even if I wanted to, because Chiffon took my bag with all the money I had to my name. I figured carrying my valuables on my person would be much safer than leaving them in the apartment, just in case the landlord got in somehow.

So after treating my black eye with ice and inspecting the black & blue marks all over my arms and stomach, I decided to call Manny in last resorts.

"Hello...?" Manny answered in a groggy voice, since I woke him up that Sunday morning.

"Boo you still sleep?" I uttered shyly.

"Who dis'?" He asked.

"I'm sorry bay-bee" I propound as if I really wanted Manny back, "I missed you... you still mad at me Man?"

"*Mende?*" Manny questioned in shock, "what the fuck you callin' me for?"

"Yeah it's me baby. I called to apologize for what happened boo boo. You were on my mind and I just want to let you know that I had nothing to do with what went down that day...I told that nigga you were my boyfriend, but he said if I didn't leave with him he'd kill me...and you too! I was so'ooo scared," I said before crying crocodile tears over the phone.

"You can save all that shit for the next nigga" Manny sneered like he was about to hang up the phone.

"No wait! What can I do to prove to you that I ain't fuckin' wit' that son of a bitch no more?"

"If you really ain't have nothin' to do wit' it like you said, then tell me where this dead man lives. I wanna' know where he rests his head."

"Well I don't know the address, but I know what the house looks like," I answered in reprieve, "If I take you there is that cool?"

"That's even better" Manny said, "be home around ten tonight. I'll pick you up and we gonna' go pay this cat a visit."

After I hung up the phone I felt reassured that I would get my revenge some way or another. To Duane I was just some jump off with a fat ass and profitable drug connections, so why not add devious devil bitch to his outlook of who I was.

Regardless of how Manny planned on

handling Duane, I didn't want to live in the hood no more. I had enough with black folks. I wished that I still had the privileges of being a regular white girl. Most of my family had cut me off when they found out I dated niggers, so there was no turning to them.

I packed my bags for wherever I was going, but before I snuck out the building, I had to stop by my brother's house first. He never got back to me about my share of the insurance money all this time. Chad and that insurance money was basically my only hope of skipping town with some doe in my pocket.

"*Tap Tap Tap*" I lightly knocked on my neighbor's door.

"Who is it?" MS. Walker answered.

"It's Mende grandma," I whispered.

"Who?"

"Mende from next door" I had to speak up.

Naturally Ms. Walker wasn't really my grandmother, but she was like a mother to everyone who lived in the apartment building. Even though she was an old black woman from the south who at one time had to let the master's children suckle her breast instead of her own children, Ms. Walker treated white people kind nonetheless. Getting up there in age Ms. Walker was losing her sight and was now unable to drive. Inconsiderate tenants would take advantage of her kindness and borrow her car to do whatever they wanted to do, but I was just going to drop by my brother's spot real quick then return her car.

"Hey Ms. Walker, I was wondering if you needed anything from the store? And I also wanted to know if I can use your car for a minute?"

"Sure sweetie, just make sure you put some gas in the car and if it's not any trouble can you pick me up a new TV guide?" Ms. Walker asked, as if the favor was on me.

"No problem I'll be back in a few."

When I got to Chad's house he was watering the lawn with one eye closed and had a cigarette hanging from his lip. He smiled suspiciously as I parked Ms. Walker's 1979 Gremlin station wagon in his three car garage driveway.

"What happened to your face," Chad frowned when I stepped out the car with a black eye and a LV scarf on my head.

"Honey is *that* your sister? Asked the woman who was kneeled down in the garden pulling up weeds.

"What's that shit supposed to mean Chad! You better check your bitch at the door" I retorted as he made his way over to greet me.

"Calm down. She's not used to nigger lovers" he laughed and snorted like a pig, "look at you Patricia you look like hell turned over! They kicked you in the ass and sent you home didn't they?"

"Fuck you Chad. What happened to the insurance money is the real question?"

"Huh?" Chad looked away still giggling to himself.

"What's up with the fucking money? It's been a long time and I need it. Why haven't you returned any of my calls" I insisted he answer me.

"Um, look we need to talk about that" Chad heaved a sigh, "I um...I...hey guess what sis? I'm getting married!" He broke out with sudden joy, "Kelly wants to travel the Caribbean first and you have to see the ring I bought...honey come show her your ring."

I walked away leaving him and Kelly standing there as he rambled off silly excuses about how and why he spent my money on her goddamn 10 carat diamond ring. Before leaving the premises never to return again, I drove Ms. Walker's Gremlin onto the lawn where I then floored the gas. The spinning tires destroyed Chad's detailed landscaping. I kept doing donuts all through the soggy lawn, which splattered mud all over the place. Chad and his stuck-up bitch were left looking like two stupid assholes with mud on their faces by the time I let up off the gas pedal.

"Con-grad-u-fuckin-lations" I shouted out the window before speeding off the property, "I hope you both die on your honeymoon!"

I was mad as hell and really counted on that insurance money to hold me down for a couple of months. Ironically my closet stored over $50,000 worth of shoes and clothes in it that I couldn't return, and my cell phone bill was in the hundreds about to be turned off. Besides all that and the landlord sweating me for the four months rent I owed, I had a rising drug habit. From doing recreational lines with Duane at house parties, cocaine had become my run-to drug. With Duane I sniffed and smoked for free, but not anymore.

Tears streamed from my contact-less blue eyes as I sat waiting at a light. Instead of returning Ms. Walker's car like I promised, I swung by the projects and copped some blow with the last bit of change in my pocket.

"*Are you gonna' let one good ass whooping chase you away that easy?*" A voice popped into my head, "Y*ou know where Duane's stash is at... rob his ass for what he did to you. You deserve it Mende.*"

Scene Eight:

The hour of chaos

When Manny picked me up I was so wired off coke, that it felt like my eyes were taped open. Even though it was dark outside I wore a leopard print scarf and some big ass Chanel shades to cover my bruised face. As I attempted to throw my bag of clothes in the back, two cats with big guns in their laps and fat blunts in their mouths, greeted me uncouthly.

"Hurry up trick! Get your pale ass in the car before you let out all the smoke" one of them uttered, "and throw that shit in the front.

"You didn't tell me you were bringing people with us baby?"

"Just shut up and get in the car!" Manny grumbled.

Manny glanced at my peculiar garb then shook his head. He snatched off my glasses then tilted my chin to examine my face.

"He did you good didn't he" Manny

commented after seeing the bruises, "just show me where the house is," he shoved my face away in disgust.

When we ultimately found Duane's house no one was home. There were no cars in the driveway and all the lights were off. Chiffon was probably staying at her father's house now, so we waited for Duane to show up. An hour later the security gate to D-R's driveway opened. Duane slowly pulled through in his Bentley. The two dudes in the backseat hopped out quietly before the iron gate closed.

As Duane drunkenly wobbled out of the car Manny and his crew jogged up the driveway with pistols dangling from their hands. Duane didn't see them. I got out of the car duplicating their sneaky steps and by the time I made it to the garage, Manny and his boys had Duane spread out on the hood of his ride like the police making an arrest.

"If you don't stop squirming you gonna' get it right here!" said the tall one with dreads, before he pistol-whipped Duane in the back of the head.

"Take his punk ass in the house!" Manny ordered.

Duane was out cold and while Manny sat on the couch aiming his .45 at him in case he woke up all of sudden, the other two dudes and I ransacked the house for anything of value.

Unlike them I knew what I was looking for and headed straight for the bedroom. When

Duane and I got drunk in the tub, he slipped up and told me where some of his money was hidden. He said he had a safe in the house, but didn't say where. What he did tell me was that he hid some of his money in the bottom dresser draw before sending it to the cleaners.

There was also a pair of diamond stick earrings in Chiffon's jewelry box I just had to have too. So while going through her shit I stumbled upon a giant pink V.V.S cut diamond ring that had to be worth a fortune by itself.

"Yo y'all find anything?" Manny yelled from downstairs.

"Nah I found a couple ounces of weed, but no doe yet," his boy hollered back.

"How bout' you Mende?" Manny inquired loudly, "anything?"

I didn't know what to say as I stood in front of what looked like a million dollars.

"Nope!" I yelled back after stuffing my pockets with as many knots as I could.

Seconds after stuffing a couple of grams of coke in my bra, Manny's two friends rushed into the bedroom with merriment on their faces when they seen all the loot in the bottom dresser drawer.

"Oh shit! We're RE'OTCH BE'OTCH!" the short one with gold fronts yelled, imitating David Chappelle as he pushed me out the way.

One of them held open an empty pillowcase, while the other dumped the entire drawer of cash into it. They might have noticed the lumps in my pocket I don't know and didn't care. We all scurried downstairs into the living room, where Duane was conscious now. He was strapped to a lazy boy with duct tape around his face and chest.

Manny peeled the tape from Duane's mouth so he could say his last words.

"I don't think y'all know who you're fuckin' wit'!" Duane proclaimed, "All you muthafucka's is dead! Especially you Mende!" he threatened before spitting at me, "Dead! Ya' heard! Dead!"

Manny's boys took turns slapping Duane around and after busting his face with a bar stool Manny pulled out his burner.

"What am I supposed to do with this?" I asked naively as Manny handed me his gun.

All the while I knew what he wanted me to do.

"What'chu think" Manny plopped back down on the couch, "pop his ass and prove to me that you hate this nigga like you said. Don't you wanna' make me happy?"

I wanted to say "*no stupid, I'm just using your dumb ass*" but I didn't.

Duane could barley talk with his mouth split open now, but amazingly he still kept mumbling shit about what he was going to do if he got free. I stood in front of Duane trembling. Manny lifted the barrel to Duane's head for me with his finger. I don't know why, but stabbing my father in the back was much easier for some reason? Even though I wanted to get back at

Duane for beating my ass and humiliating me, I really did love him.

Manny and his crew turned up the pressure by cheering me on to squeeze the trigger.

"*Do it! Do it!*" they all yelled as if I was in college chugging down a beer, "*Do that shit! Go! Go! Go! Go!*"

I closed my eyes and tried to fire, but nothing happened. I squeezed it again and still nothing. Everyone laughed feverishly as the joke was obviously on me. My heart was pounding and I even had sweat on my brow. Manny had given me an empty gun and just wanted to see if I would pull the trigger.

"Yo you owe me fifty bucks" Manny shouted to his boy, "I told you that bitch got it in her...I seen the killer in her cold blue eyes."

I was pissed. My back was soaked with perspiration and my hands were still shaking. I think if there had actually been bullets in that gun, I would've just shot Manny and his friends then bounced.

"*BLOOM! BLOOM!*" Two shots unexpectedly fired.

Without warning the dude with the dreads shot Duane in the chest at point blank range. The other one with the gold teeth snatched the empty gun from me, and then slapped me on my ass with it as he pushed me to the door.

"How much you think we got?" Manny asked all excited.

"A lot nigga, just keep drivin'" Dread answered as if he was in control the whole time.

It was evident that Manny's two so-called friends didn't respect him and it made me real nervous. They kept looking at me whispering to each other in the backseat. Something didn't feel right.

"Yo Manny, pull over right here." Dread uttered as we passed a dark alley.

"For what?" Manny answered hot and bothered.

"Man just pull over...I gotta' take a piss" he complained.

When Manny pulled over Dread got out and his boy stayed seated in the back. I was extremely tense with my hand on the door the entire time. No sooner than I turned around to look in the backseat a gun was pointed to my head.

"*Click...Click*"

I thought I was dead, but the gun didn't fire. That stupid bastard tried to kill me with the same empty gun he took away from me back at the house. He struggled to switch guns, but by the time he did I was gone.

"Boom! Boom! Boom!" Dread fired three shots into Manny's head from outside of the car.

"Get that bitch!" He yelled.

I was already halfway down the street before they even realized it. Even though I felt a strong burning sensation in my back and stomach, I kept on running until I saw crowds of people. Who knew I could run so fast. When I hit the corner I dashed into Dunkin' Donuts and collapsed on the floor. Customers screamed when they seen all the blood on my clothes and some of them even came over to help me, if you call taking everything out of my pockets help. They took everything including, Chiffon's jewelry on my neck, wrist and fingers, plus the doe.

Five minutes later the ambulance came and I was rushed to Saint Raphael Hospital. My clothes were cut off of my body with huge scissors as the nurses checked for more bullet holes. When I awoke hours later a young female doctor greeted me. My body was still aching from Duane and Chiffon's beat down and now it felt like a truck had ran over it. To top it all off the fucking police had cuffed me to the bedrail. I struggled to get free for a minute then sunk back into the bed out of breath.

"I have good news and some bad news for you" the pencil neck doctor stated in her East Indian accent.

She took my blood pressure and wrote something on the chart.

"Oh really? What?" I asked in total agony.

"The good news is that you're going to live. Your body is still in shock and you'll be sore for weeks to come of course, but you're going to make it. The bullet exited the side of your abdomen and tore a few vital organs, but we took care of the damage."

I was glad, but the sorrowful look on the

doctor's face puzzled me.

"The bad news is...there was nothing we could do I'm so sorry...you lost the baby."

"What baby?" I started sobbing.

"You didn't know that you were two months pregnant?" The doctor asked oddly, "It looks like your body went into shock causing terminal stress on the fetus."

I couldn't stop crying. No one else but God knew how much I wanted to have a baby one day, but I didn't even know I was carrying. All those times I threw up in the morning I just thought it was from a bad hangover from the night before and never considered the cause being morning sickness. With all the raw dog sex we had, it had to be Duane's.

"I really am sorry," said the doctor, "but I have some more bad news. There's an officer in the hall ready to take you into custody as soon as your I.V is complete."

"For what!" I yelled at her, "I'm the one that fucking got shot bitch! I just lost my fucking baby!" I screamed uncontrollably trying to kick at her while cuffed to the bed.

"Please calm down ma'am I'm just doing my job. If you cooperate I can see that you stay here tonight instead of going to jail. It's procedure to notify the police of any type of shooting and illegal drugs were found on your person, so there's not much I can do if you scream and yell."

At the time I didn't know that a nurse in

the emergency room found a few little bags of coke in my bra when they cut my clothes off.

"That's Bullshit! I'll slap that red dot off your head if you don't un-cuff me right now!" I yelled.

"*Officers...*" the doctor scowled as the two cops entered the room, "take it up with them...*can you remove this woman at once please.*"

Any other girl would have lost it too, if she had just lost a life growing inside of her that she knew nothing about and never mind the fact of not having a damn thing to her name, when she had it all.

I regretted taking things out on the doctor, because she was just trying to help me out. The price was going to jail wounded and stressed. On the ride down to the New Haven police station, I made myself feel grateful by stressing the thought that I at least escaped death and would hopefully escape a murder charge for the second time.

"*You have reached Chad and Kelly we're not home right now...*"

I used my only phone call to call my brother Chad to see if he would bail me out, but the fucking answering machine came on.

"UUUUGGGHHH!" I sighed in irritation.

I was so frustrated that the police had to stop me from repeatedly slamming the phone against the cell wall.

The next morning I felt even more pitiful at

the arraignment, because my bond was only
$1000, which meant I only had to come up with
10% ($100) and I didn't even have that. All my
money was gone and I was going to have to stay
in jail until my next court date. Since females
were not allowed to stay in the Whalley Avenue
county jail I was expecting to be shipped
upstate, which was the moment I feared.

Scene Nine:
The hate that love produced

Around the same time when I killed my father, there was a beautiful young girl seventy miles out of Connecticut, bumping people off for virtuous reasons. Unlike me, Kali loved and missed her pops dearly. To die in place of someone you love is the true warrior's premise, and Kali's father Tawi, was a true warrior no doubt.

Tawi was the leader of a vigilante group out of Brooklyn, New York. They called themselves the VETS, since each member was a Vietnam veteran. The VETS were trained killing machines in Nam and killing machines when they returned from the war. Some people disagreed with their method of cleaning up the streets, but in retrospect the VETS only killed for what they believed in, which was "Protect your family at all cost."

While Kali's father was up to his ass in bullets and rice paddies overseas, her mother began experimenting with cocaine. Mrs. Hunter eventfully became a full-fledged crack head and seemed to forget that she had a little girl to raise. She stayed out all night suckin' and fuckin' for a ten second high. Kali's father was totally disgusted and heartbroken. By the time Kali made it to high school, her parents officially divorced. Tawi fought for custody of Kali, but lost in the gender biased family court. He knew that his ex-wife would use the child support money to cop drugs, instead of using it to take care of Kali.

Time went on and Kali would stop by her father's apartment everyday before school to eat breakfast. She would also stop by afterwards to eat dinner too, regardless of who was her legal guardian. Since Kali's mother neglected to give a shit, her father gave a quality effort to teach her how to be a woman the best way he knew how.

Tawi schooled his baby girl about sex and drugs and how to defend herself against anyone who grabbed her inappropriately. Being the ruthless soldier that he was, Tawi's parenting program graduated from basic boxing lessons to assault riffle training. By age 16 Kali developed a mean right hook and knew how to disarm the average gun-toter in the projects. She could also snipe a target from 100 yards away and carried a weapon on her person at all times. Identical to how her father mastered the martial arts, Kali too had become a patron of warfare. It was just a matter of time before she started taking people out.

People gathered in droves surrounding Tawi Hunter's ultimate resting place at Evergreen Cemetery. Standing tall at the funeral service were muscular Vietnam veterans, most in their 50's and 60's, positioned in the vein of honor guards. For Tawi's final send off a local jazz band blew shiny brass horns and trumpets in a New Orleans fashion. Their instruments blared with melodic intensity as Birds in nearby trees flew away as one. Kali's eyes filled with tears, but she still stood firm.

Kali's best friend Ma'ati consoled her tightly as the men lowered her father's casket into the Earth. Neither of them said a word. Ma'ati and Kali just stared off in different directions. They held each other, reflecting the lives of their father's who both went down protecting the ones they loved. Although Ma'ati's father wasn't actually dead, it felt as if he was, because he was doing double digits upstate in Sing Sing.

After the lengthy service finally concluded, Kali and her mother, who was now known on the streets as "Loony", exited the complementary limousine in front of the Van-Dyke housing project. Kali and her mother were rarely seen together despite the fact that Loony still had legal custody. All beefs were put on hold today, since Loony agreed to help Kali clear Tawi's stuff out of his apartment. Loony did help a little, but as soon as she found a few dollars in one of her husband's old army jacket pockets she headed out the door.

"I'll be back in a minute" Loony claimed, "I need me a cigarette."

"Whateva'" Kali thoughtlessly responded, while she carried on taping up cardboard boxes.

Loony rushed downstairs and walked right over toward the group of poison pushers that were gathered by the benches. She copped herself a blast and that was it, as far as helping. Hours later after packing everything by herself, Kali decided to find Loony and curse her out for not helping like she promised.

Using the stairs instead of the pissy elevators was custom for Kali, because her father said the elevators were a death trap. By the time Kali had got down to the 3rd floor, an echoed voice could be heard steps below.

"I'm glad Tawi's army pants wearing ass is dead" Pretty boy James professed, "now we might be able to get some good dope around this mu'fucka'! *Who in the hell did he think he was*...supernigga or somethin'?"

Kali was infuriated at the disrespect coming from this dudes mouth, but she held her tongue and took a seat on the steps to listen. The person talking junk was Pretty Boy James, a local crack head/part time dealer that got high with Loony time to time before the VETS shut shit down. Matter of fact James was the one who turned Loony on to drugs when Kali's father was on tour in Vietnam.

"Boy close yo mouth and unzip 'dem pants," Loony bickered, "I don't wanna' hear 'dat shit right now?"

Being that Loony didn't have enough money for all of the crack Pretty boy James smoked with her, she agreed to suck him off on the staircase in return. Kali recognized her mother's voice and became totally enraged like never before. She ran back up the stairs grabbing the first weapon in sight. On the bathroom sink sat a straight razor her father used to shave with and the next thing you know, Kali was running back down the steps with it in her grip. As Loony slurped and burped funky pink balls, Pretty boy James continued to run his mouth.

"If only Tawi could see us now?" He chuckled like the Joker.

He wouldn't be laughing much longer. Neither Pretty boy nor Loony, who was kneeling on the steps, heard Kali creep down from behind. Pretty boy James stood there looking down at Loony with his hands on his waist, before Kali pulled his head back. She wrapped his long stringy blonde hair around her palm then ferociously slit his throat. In the blink of an eye blood poured forth from Pretty Boy's neck onto her mother's head like a cheap horror movie. Pretty boy convulsed himself down the steps as Loony stared in shock at all the blood. Loony then shrieked as Pretty Boy James lay there shaking.

"Oh my fuckin' gawd Kali! What did you do! Oh my god!".

Kali silenced Loony's piercing scream by covering her mother's mouth with her hand. In seconds Pretty boy was dead with his eyes bulging out his head. Kali looked down at the body with an ice-cold stare, and then spat in his eye before she walked back up the stairs. Loony was still in disbelief, but being the crack head that she was, she went through Pretty Boy's pockets. Loony stuffed the bloody sandwich bag of rocks into her dingy dress suit pocket, before rushing up the stairs behind Kali.

"My father might be dead but his spirit lives through me" Kali declared walking gallantly up the steps, "fuck Pretty boy James and the rest of these dope pushin' vampires! I'm gonna' kill all these muthafucka's watch!"

Kali's threat sounded more like a promise. As she washed the blood off her hands, the white porcelain sink in the bathroom turned red. Loony stormed into the bathroom panicking.

"What is we gon' do?" Loony asked hysterically, in fear that someone seen what happened or heard her scream.

"I don't know 'bout you, but I'm gonna' have a piece of that pie Mrs. Geter made for us" Kali stated casually as she dried her hands on a towel.

"You must have lost your goddamn mind child! Do you know what you just did" Loony yelled after taking a nervous hit from her crack pipe, "we both goin' down for this!"

"No...you already went down remember!" Kali hollered back with tears running down her face, "Look at you! You look like a fuckin' monster smoking that shit!"

"'Day 'gon kill us I know it!" Loony repeated as the crack paranoia set in more.

"Who gonna' kill us? Don't nobody care about what happens around here!" Kali said, before slapping the pipe out of her mother's mouth, "daddy died cause you and that damn shit and you got the nerve to trick in his building for it! I hope you choke on the next dick you suck! Get the hell out my way!"

Kali collected her father's guns and other memorabilia that she wanted to keep, before leaving the apartment one last time. Loony picked up the glass stem that her daughter knocked to the floor, then sat on the couch flicking her lighter. Kali marched out the door carrying two bulky duffle bags then turned around halfway through the door.

"I never told you this before" Kali confessed standing under the threshold, "I wanted to be just like you when I was little, but now you make me sick and I hope one day, while you're layin' in the gutta' all high, you realize that you had a family who loved you."

Loony began to cry. When she couldn't get

her lighter to work, she flung her precious crack pipe in frustration. Ironically as the pipe shattered against the wall in a thousand pieces, someone else's mother was beaming up successfully on the other side of the same wall.

Pretty Boy's body was still lying in the stairwell as Kali jogged down the steps. She stepped over his lifeless body and kept it moving while thinking what to do next. Kali ended up in an empty laundromat where she decided to wash her bloody clothes. When nightfall drew closer she called up her girl Ma'ati needing to talk to someone. Ma'ati happened to be staying with her aunt Sherl for the summer only two buildings away from the laundromat.

"Hi Sherl is Ma home? I need to speak with her."

"I thought you and Loony were cleaning out your father's apartment...*that was quick* is everything okay?" Sherl asked.

"I'm i'ight" Kali sighed.

"Ma'ati went out with Laquan, but if you want, you can wait over here until she gets back."

Sherl watched Kali grow up and loved her like her own. Over the years she witnessed how ill mannered Loony treated her daughter and foreseen the tribulations heading Kali's way. Sherl was the kind of woman that teenagers felt comfortable talking to. Most young girls in Sherl's building came to her when they had problems. Sherl knew that although these girls looked grown, they were still mentally immature and needed guidance.

Ten minutes later Kali showed up at Sherl's door looking like a lost puppy.

"What's up girl?" Sherl posed with her hand on her hip as she opened the door, "you sounded so upset on the phone you sure everything's all right?"

Kali dropped her bags with a helpless stare. She needed to exhale the fire from her lungs.

"I miss my father so much" Kali let out a deep breath, "I had a big fight with my mother, cause her stupid ass crack head friend was talkin' shit..."

Before Kali could explain the rest of the story Sherl hugged her tightly then helped her with her bags. She didn't need to know the details about the fight. Kali got situated on the couch before dozing off watching TV. At 2 A.M Ma'ati finally strolled in. She was shocked to find Kali fidgeting on Sherl's sticky leather couch tossing and turning. To cool her friend off, Ma'ati turned on the noisy window fan, but it didn't work and only woke Kali up.

"About time" Kali yawned, "I was waitin' for you forever girl."

"Laquan took me to the Beacon to see one of those mama plays" Ma'ati answered as she plopped down on the couch, "he's so sweet ain't he?"

"I killed somebody" Kali just bust out and

said, "and you know what Ma? I don't even care."

Ma'ati looked befuddled as she took off her boots.

"What'chu mean you killed somebody? Who? What happened?"

"I don't know what came over me, but when I seen my mother sucking his dick then heard that motherfucka' talkin' shit about my father I just...yo I just lost it."

Kali swung the remote through the air in demonstration of how she cut PBJ's throat. Ma'ati kept quiet. She let Kali get everything off her chest.

During that awful humid night, they talked until the Sun came up. Both girls agreed that drugs changed everything for the worst in their families, but Ma'ati didn't necessarily think that they should carry on where Kali's father left off.

"I agree with you Kali somebody needs to do something around here" Ma'ati remarked as she picked lint balls from her pajamas, "but insanity is doin' the same thing everyday expecting a different result. How is killin' people gonna' change things? Every time your pops took out a dope dealer, another one took his place!"

"True" Kali replied, "but someone has to do it. Why not us?"

"You know I respect your father and what he did" Ma'ati apologized, "but we should learn from his mistakes instead of acting out of rage. It's not really how many you take out, it's who you take out."

"Now that sounds more like it" Kali winked as she curled up on the couch, "two fly ass chicks like us...they'll never see it comin'."

That morning their destiny was sealed, and soon a furious rage would sweep through the streets once again in the name of retribution. Only this time, the vigilantes would be wearing Prada and Jimmy Choo instead of army fatigues.

Scene Ten:

On the come up

Instead of graduating high school like I did, Kali and Ma'ati enrolled themselves into the School of Hard Knocks. Although street life is two-faced and heartless, there is knowledge, wisdom and understanding creeping around underneath. You just have to find it. Dug deep in the basement of an old raggedy three family house on Sutter Ave in the East New York section of BK, dwelled Johnny Red. He was somewhat of an uncle to Kali. Her father left instructions for Red to look out for his daughter if anything ever happened to him.

Johnny Red was in a wheel chair after his legs were blown off in the war, but he was still the best combat and weapons trainer around. If you ever needed a weapon Johnny Red was the man to see.

"What's up Red, this is my girl Ma'ati" Kali announced as she struggled with a heavy bag down the stairs, "I brought all the stuff from my father's house like you asked, so are you gonna' hit us off with some of that high powered shit you got down here."

"Hello little lady" Johnny Red smiled as he examined Ma'ati from head to toe, "some of history's most brilliant warriors were women did you know that? But you two look like soft school girls" he said.

"Looks are deceiving" Ma'ati simpered before Red rolled back across the basement, "and yes, we are the most brilliant warriors" she asserted.

Johnny Red spread out a wool army blanket containing the latest handguns on the market. Each Glock looked brand new and the chrome weapons shined like Canal street silver.

"Ooh I like this one!" Ma'ati grinned while examining the Desert Eagle in her hand.

"Not so fast" Johnny Red yelled out as he took the gun away from Ma, "these aren't yours...those are yours over there."

Red pointed to a dirty duffle bag filled to the top with guns that looked like they hadn't been used in years.

"What's this shit Red?" Kali complained, "I just got my nails done, come on Red we ain't come here for no rusty ass rifles!"

"Shovel the bullshit to someone else. Soldiers need to learn how to clean their own weapon. Back in Nam I-"

"Nam is over" Kali cut him off, "we just need some burners man."

"You girls are gonna' have to learn some discipline! Nothing in this world is for free! After you clean these old guns I'll give you the new ones. If that means breaking every goddamn nail on your fingers then that's what it means. Now get to work or get to steppin'!"

Kali and Ma sucked their teeth, but did as Red instructed. It took about three weeks to clean all of Johnny Red's weapons in his approved manner, but by the time the girls were finished, they could dismantle and assemble any gun in their sleep. Red worked them like the soldiers they aspired to be and in just a matter of months, Kali and Ma'ati graduated to disciplining themselves.

Both girls gained an infamous rep around the way for taking no shit. With fatal charm and a cache of weapons at arms reach, Kali was more lethal than ever. Troublemakers had a funny way of disappearing after getting on her bad side. Like an elephant never forgets, Kali remembered all the people that sold her mother drugs and killed them one by one.

Instead of wasting time on insignificant street hustlers who sold poison for a petty profit, Ma'ati convinced her partner that it was wiser to hit the big timers, since they were the ones who actually supplied the streets.

On their first big hit Kali and Ma entered

an apartment hallway where a brand of dope stamped *New York's Finest* was sold. It was some powerful dope, even more potent than China White. Fiends were dying all over from it, which made it sell all the more. Me being a cokehead and all, I never really understood why someone would want to buy some drugs that you know can kill you on the spot. Where's the fun it that?

"You ready?" Kali whispered.

"As much as I'm gonna' be" Ma responded before concealing her identity.

Little did they know that they were seconds away from going up against the boys in blue. The ski masks on their faces and assault weapons in their grips caused the dope fiends waiting in line to scurry. They kicked in the door like stick up kids with a vengeance, shooting shit up until no more shots were fired back.

As for the two addicts that stood behind the riddled door, their morning heartaches were now over. Bulletproof vests didn't helped out much for the ones guarding the front room, because both girls packed AR-15's with 3 extra sets of clips containing hollow tipped rounds. When the dope powdered smoke cleared Ma'ati' looked surprised.

"Oh shit!" She said, "look! They're fuckin' cops!""

Unexpectedly two police lieutenants were caught in the middle of counting their weekly profits and laid there dead on top of the cash.

Pasta bowls and dope were scattered all over the kitchen table. The apartment was basically vacant except for a 13-inch Television set, a couch and kitchen cabinets that stored pounds of dope and tons of cash. Between the two of them, Kali and Ma'ati had eliminated a small team of crooked cops that were moving serious heroin throughout Brooklyn, unintentionally.

While Kali stuffed cash in a book bag, Ma'ati dumped the drugs in the sink and filled it with water. There was so much money laying around, that Kali had to leave most of it behind. With more than $100,000 in singles, fives, and tens, they fled the building unscathed and unseen.

Everybody knows when black people get money they start acting funny and it can easily overshadow any moral purpose. Ma'ati realized that if they didn't put the dirty money to good use, they would be just as corrupt and bloodthirsty as the ones they took it from. Kali agreed, so later Ma'ati devised ways to make the doe work in the hood's favor. Besides funding a handful of grassroots organizations, Ma'ati donated thousands to after school programs that were cut by the state.

However, they spared no expense on themselves to keep up with the illusion of being fashion stylists in the music industry. Normally if you start driving new cars and wearing expensive clothes, without a source of income, it looks hot. Fronting like they were part of the booming music business was a good disguise. Everyone in the projects knew Ma'ati's boyfriend Laquan had a record deal, so they just assumed that Ma'ati was getting hers that way too.

A few weeks after the big score, the girls got news of a friend sent to the hospital. Kali drove through Brooklyn itching to fuck somebody up and it didn't take long before she spotted the person she was looking for.

"Is that that sorry excuse of a man?" Kali uttered as she hit the brakes before circling down Junis Ave.

"Yeah that's Millz" Ma'ati confirmed, "he used to pump weed out'a Bristol Park, but now he moved up to crack. He's a real asshole."

"We should get his ass right now for what he did to Toya" Kali exploded with bitterness, "this is the fifth time he sent her to emergency over some bullshit. You think he's holdin' heat?" Kali asked.

"More than likely," Ma answered, "I know he's got mad beef wit' niggas, so he's probably strapped."

As they watched Millz step out of his Lexus coupe, Kali inserted a clip into her 9mm before she got out the car.

The dude about to get it dated her girl Toya. Toya used to roll with Kali and another wild crew called the *Buck Fifty Bitches*, due to the 150 stitches they usually left on people's faces with their box cutters. That was some time ago, but the more things change, the more they stay the same.

Toya's boyfriend Millz used to play ball overseas, but after breaking his ankle on the court he resorted to pushing crack when he returned to the States. Millz was very possessive and beat Toya's ass whenever he felt like it. He slapped her around for just about anything. This time he put Toya in the hospital with a broken jaw after noticing an unfamiliar number on her cell, which happened to be Kali calling.

Millz had disappeared into his apartment building then came back out ten minutes later carrying a small travel bag. His long white T-shirt fit more like a skirt and from the protrusion around his waist it was obvious that he was strapped. Kali sat on the trunk of his car like she had his keys in her pocket. The streetlights beamed a glare off of her shiny black thighs, which captured Millz attention for a minute. It was as if Kali heard his sexual thoughts. The squint in her eye revealed extreme dislike and when Millz got closer he tried to match Kali's ice grill.

"Do I know you?" Millz hollered like he didn't appreciate Kali all up on his Benz.

Kali just shrugged her shoulders as she licked her lollypop with little concern. Although Millz was up in her face talking shit, she just ignored him and kept conversing on her cell.

"I know you hear me talkin' to you bitch" Millz sneered, "get off my shit right now!"

"S'cuse me? What'chu just say?" Kali

tossed her lollypop to the side.

Before Millz could yank Kali off his car, Ma'ati crept up from behind and slapped him in the face with a tire iron. Kali grabbed Millz around the waist quickly removing his gun, and then she karate kicked him in the back. The forceful punt caused Millz' head to hit the front bumper of the car parked behind his, before he fell backwards on the curb.

"Lay down and stay down!" Kali yelled while she held Millz own gun to his head.

She then placed her cell phone to his ear to relay a cordial message from Toya.

"Fuuggkk yoouuggh Mrrillss" Toya muddled through the phone.

Being that Toya's mouth was wired shut, her words came out garbled, but Millz still recognized the voice and his face just dropped in regret.

"Smile for the camera asshole...*POW!*" Kali shot him once in the kneecap, "that's for calling me a bitch!"

Millz screamed like a coyote in excruciating pain. They fucked that nigga up. No more triple doubles at street ball events for him. He probably wouldn't even be able to walk straight again.

"Now this one's for Toya" Ma'ati bellowed before smacking him with the tire iron once more...*PLUNK!*

The last blow was solid. It smashed Millz jaw like a piece of glass. Kali used her videophone to transmit the whole thing directly to Toya's cell, while she laid in the emergency room. An eye for an eye or rather a jaw for a jaw made this one even as they left Millz squirming in the gutter.

On the way to visit Toya Kali dropped by Ma'ati's sister's house to give her a ride to work. Ma's sister Michelle was a RN who worked at the Hospital where Toya was admitted. As they walked through the doors that led to Triage, laughter could be heard. When Kali pulled back the curtain she was greeted by Riva and Jackie, two other members from her old click.

"What's really good wit'chu" Riva addressed Kali, "damn Ma...you got thick as hell girl what'chu been eatin'?"

Seconds later a wrinkled old nurse threatened to have them all removed because it got so loud up in there.

"This is a hospital not a nightclub" the woman said, "if you can't keep it down I will have you all removed!"

They ignored the crabby nurse and exchanged hugs like old friends do. After 15 minutes of reminiscing it was time to go.

"We just stopped by to see how you were doing" Ma'ati said while giving Toya a hug goodbye, "Shell told me that she'll see you on her break."

"So what do y'all bitches be doin' these days?" Riva jealously inquired before they left, "you got all fancy on us all of a sudden...wrist blingin' and shit? Drivin' new whips every month. I heard you be pickin' out clothes for rappers now. When you gonna' put us on?" Riva waited for an answer.

"Yeah those rocks look sick" Jackie examined Kali's wrist, "what's that about 5 carats?"

"I gotta' go but I'll tell you what" Kali let Jackie stare, "round up the twins and meet us at Junior's tomorrow night around eight. I have a proposition for you if you're interested."

The next day 8:00 came around. Riva, Jackie, Toya and the twins Nika and Mika, congregated outside of Junior's restaurant in downtown Brooklyn, until Kali and Ma'ati pulled up in a brand new shiny Hummer. Jealousy filled Riva's eye, but she played it off and smiled like the rest of her friends.

The crew's entrance pulled on everyone's attention like the Moon does the tide. Ma'ati had on a sexy white lace bustier under a black leather motorcycle vest with skin tight Jeans. Kali walked around from the driver side in a pair of leather shorts that complemented her heart shaped behind. Her firm-cupped breasts slightly moved side to side in the spaghetti strap top she wore as she made her way to the table.

"I'm glad you all made it" Kali said as she slid into the booth next to Riva, "here's the deal. All of you knew my pops and the things he did. Who could forget all them shootouts, but I got a way for us to get paid and help out the community at the same time like he did."

"Doin' what?" Jackie asked, "God knows I'm tired of gettin' followed around the stores while Riva boosts us somethin' to wear to the club."

Riva kicked Jackie's foot under the table before she said anything else. Jackie always gave too much information when she talked.

"Basically we're retiring anyone who gets on the shit list!" Kali answered, "You know, like the drug dealers that sell crack to pregnant woman and shoot little kids over short packages."

"And if you think it's all about the money your wrong. It's about picking up where her father left off" Ma'ati added, "what we take we put back into the hood."

"Get the fuck out'a here" Riva retorted sucking her teeth, "you pulled up in a brand new Hummer and we pulled up on the fuckin' D train! I don't know bout' yall" Riva scanned the other girl's faces, "but I wanna' get paid. Fuck dat' righteous shit!"

"Chill Riva...listen first before you start runnin' off at the mouth" Ma'ati angrily replied.

"Yeah bitch zip it! Listen to what the fuck she gotta' say before you start complaining" one of the twins intervened, "they're tryna' put us on, so shut the fuck up! Go ahead Kali finish what you were saying."

Kali stood up and pulled out five jewelry boxes from her pink Coach bag.

"Don't get it twisted, there's rules to this shit and my heart is in this so watch yourself Riva. What did we get out of runnin' wit' BFB? Nothin' but scars and court cases. Don't you wanna' step ya' game up? I know all about your lil' credit card scams and rip offs girl, we grown ass women now c'mon."

"Where exactly does the money go?" the other twin Nika asked, "and what makes you think we can't go to jail or get killed?" Her sister joined in.

"As far as the money is concerned," Ma'ati replied, "some of it goes into a savings fund for each of us, and since a sista' gotta' look good, some of it goes in your pocket. But most of the money goes to organizations in the hood that really need the funds. I even put together a few organizations myself and we've been helping the halfway houses and shelters out too. One of the programs that I created was S.E.E.D.S. It's a program that helps children stay in touch with their parents or family members when they're locked up. We hit children off with money for clothes and food or any other things unavailable to them while their parents are upstate. This keeps a lifeline going" Ma said, "It doesn't let prison sever families like it's intended to do. I know there's much more that could be done, but for now it's at least a start."

"And to answer your question Mika I can only promise you loyalty. I can't promise you that you won't get killed or go to jail" Kali cracked her knuckles, "that's the risk you have to take if you join, but I can train you to be the most deadliest chick with a gun that the streets has ever seen."

After every question was answered, Kali slid each girl a jewelry box with an initialized WH diamond bracelet inside.

"The WH stands for your new family *the Woman Hood*. If you accept this gift there's no turning back" Kali made clear as she watched each person's reaction, "that means never betray anyone at this table or take from anybody in the streets that don't deserve it. If you break these rules that's your ass! And I mean it."

All the girls at the table seemed excited except Riva. Riva felt that if she was going to rob and kill people why not keep 100% of everything.

"*Who the fuck does Kali think she is?*" Riva thought to herself with a smirk on her face.

"You in or out?" Ma'ati put Riva on the spot, as she sat there looking up at the ceiling.

"I don't know...I'm just not feelin' the idea of givin' up half my doe for some shit I don't believe in. Can you give me some time to think about this thing," Riva asked with no intention of abiding by any set of laws.

"You got a week to make up your mind" Kali retracted the box sitting in front of Riva. She then turned her attention to the other girls, "from this point on we all work as one unit..."

While the rest of the crew tried on their new Woman Hood bracelets, Riva bit into her cheesecake looking disjointed as she thought about her decision.

"They got rules and I got rules too...fuck everybody else cause I'm gonna' do me!"

Riva left things in the air and never got back to Kali with her final decision. About a week later she was up to her old ways again, despite Jackie's advice to leave the petty boosting alone. Riva didn't listen.

A few days later Riva along with some other dumb bitch, fled all the way to the Stamford train station with thousands of dollars in stolen clothes. The security team from Saks Fifth Avenue chased them out the Mall, but lost them in the rush hour crowds. A Good Samaritan joined in the pursuit and fingered Riva as she ducked behind commuters waiting for the train. The other girl wasn't that dumb because she got away, but Riva got knocked. She struggled with the Metro police officers until a box cutter fell out of her bag.

"Don't move!" Officers closed in on her, "freeze!"

Riva was finished. Being that she had a blade and fought back scratching and kicking, the police trumped up the charges to assault with a deadly weapon on top of the grand larceny charges that she faced. In a little while Riva would meet yours truly, known for the time being as inmate number 407112.

Scene Eleven:

Bullpen therapy

I never thought the day would come when I would be glad to be in prison, but doing time upstate was much better than sleeping in filthy ass county jail. This was my fifth month in the York Correctional Institution and my last days were finally approaching. I only had 684 hours left to go and I couldn't wait to get the fuck out of there. I think I could've beat the charges, but my public defender, or should I say public pretender, convinced me that I would lose if I fought the case, so I copped out to a possession charge. If I had money for a real liar, I mean lawyer, I know I could've just got probation.

"Yo white girl" a familiar face shouted as I walked passed a table of chicks playing cards, "Yo I'm talkin' to you snow white...you wanna' play spades or you too good to play cards?"

I looked around like *I know she ain't*

129

talking to me, because nobody ever asked me to play anything.

"What are you deaf?" Riva tugged on my shirt, "I don't see no other white girls walkin' 'round here...you wanna' play or what?"

During the entire five months in prison I hadn't talked to anyone except the C.O's. Everybody in there thought I was strange and usually left me alone because I talked to myself out loud. For some reason Riva acted different.

Whenever it rained outside, my bullet wounds would ache, so I walked over to the table holding my side.

"Okay I'll play."

"Grab a seat cabro'na'" the two Puerto Rican girls laughed with each other.

"Let's see if it's funny when we set your asses" Riva spoke up in our defense as I sat down.

Riva didn't look like she belonged in prison until she opened her mouth. She was a real feisty one. However her appearance was still totally feminine. She looked a lot like Christina Milian, just a little darker and much more thugged out. It was obvious by the way she talked that Riva was a hard rock. When she stood her legs arched back in such a sexy way, which I thought was appealing. Riva bragged that she was down for 10 months already and had two months left like me.

"So where you from" I began the conversation as Riva dealt out the cards, "you from New Haven?"

"Hell no I'm from Buck town baby...Brooklyn if you don't know" Riva raised her voice as she slammed down an ace of spade, "I got knocked on some larceny bullshit in Stamford, but a gun fell out my bag and the muthafucka's hit me wit' assault wit' a deadly weapon...can you believe that shit!"

After winning two games straight, Riva and I hit the showers before count time. Even though we shared the same cube, we had never really spoke until now. While Riva closed her eyes to block out the soap, the water bounced off of her perky breasts. I watched the bubbles follow each curve down to the back of her leg. I scanned her picturesque body from head to toe before rubbing my box in a circular motion fantasizing us in a 69.

Riva was beautiful point blank. I wanted her bad. Losing the baby and thinking about how Duane shit on me fucked up my head. Dick was no longer the highlight of my life. I don't know if it was from psychological trauma or what, but my attraction for men had gradually started to fade. I now found women more appealing, but I admit that I still craved a good dick every now and then.

When Riva noticed what I was doing she looked at me with a puckered smile. Those tantalizing lips of hers drove me wild.

"Damn girl you got some big ass knockers" Riva smiled again, "are they yours?" She asked, while wrapping a towel around herself.

"I guess so...I paid for 'em right?" I returned the same enticing gaze, "go ahead you can squeeze 'em if you want to Riva don't be *scurred*" we both giggled.

Just as Riva was about to tweak my nipples, in walked two disgusting gargantuan looking bitches. Self-conscious about how it looked I guess, Riva rushed back to the sink. I finished drying off as the fat Kirsty Alley looking twins surrounded me.

"How much did these shits cost" the ugliest one out of the two asked as she grabbed my breasts really hard, "they feel like Nerf balls."

"Get your fat hands off me" I pulled away backing into Riva, who was now brushing her hair in the mirror.

Everyday during lunch these same two whales tried to take my food. If I didn't give it to them they stuck boogers in it so I wouldn't eat it. This time one of them had a disposable razor in her hand. The other stood there looking me up and down as she lit a cigarette from the arc of the light bulb socket.

See in prison bitches fuck with you when they find out you're about to go home. They figure they could do anything to you and you won't fight back, because you might jeopardize your freedom if you get a ticket. Given that Riva was discharging, that theory didn't apply to her. Without any delay Riva turned around and smacked girl one with a sock full of AA batteries that she had hidden under her towel. Riva kept hitting the girl until she saw blood. Girl two seen her friend fall to the floor and took off running like a punk.

"Kick that hoe in her head," Riva commanded as I stomped the bitch's face in.

Just as I got into kicking her ass, *"RECALL, RECALL FOR COUNT"* sounded over the loud speaker.

"Yo a C.O's comin' lets be out," Riva stopped me from going off.

We both hurried to our cube while fatso laid on the shower floor holding her eye. They never messed with me again and since that day I felt like I owed Riva something for sticking up for me. I stuck to her like glue for the rest of my bid. I even thought that I was falling in love with her.

On an early Saturday morning while everyone else was sleep including the guards, I led Riva into the bathroom. I wanted to show her how much I enjoyed her company.

"What'chu gotta' show me Mende I'm goin' back to sleep girl" Riva whispered, "it's five-thirty in the morning."

"Let me taste you" I uttered softly, "even your touch excites me," I panted heavy while pulling on her sweat pants.

Riva was shocked at how forward I was. I made her sit down on the cold toilet seat then forced her legs up. Her feet pressed against the sides of the stall as I went down on her. For this being my first time giving a chick head, it felt natural. Her pink sugar melted in my mouth like cotton candy.

It was dead quiet and the sounds of me lapping labia and clitoris echoed in the bathroom. Riva tasted like a peach soaked in syrup and I consumed each drop as her legs began to shake. Her wetness leaked into my nostrils as booty juice glazed my face. I made her taste herself with a French kiss then afterwards we traipsed back to our cube holding hands.

For hours I listened to Riva tell me stories about how her girls back home were getting paid robbing drug dealers. I thought I was wild, but Riva had me beat with the stories she told. Up until the last night of my sentence, I hadn't cried once until then.

"So what'chu gonna' do when you get out'a here" I asked Riva, "I wish I had someone to go home to, I don't know what I'm gonna' do?"

As the tears began to stream down my cheek, Riva held me close to her chest then caught herself, like she was too hard to share emotions.

"I'll punch you in your face if you don't stop crying Mende...look here, I'll be in Connecticut for a lil' while, then I'm goin' back to Brooklyn. You can stay with me for a couple of days until you get right. Now will you stop crying like a lil' bitch someone might see us."

"Would you really do that for me?" I perked up, "I'll make it worth your while I promise Riva!

All I need to do is find me a job then I'm straight!"

The next morning I got up extra early anxious to be released. I left everything in my locker. Anyone who wanted those nasty Ramien soups and concord jelly bottles could have them. After waiting through one more head count the list of names were called to the AP room over the loud speaker. Unlike Riva I still had probation hanging over my head and needed someone to sign me out. Thank god Riva's cousin agreed to do it or my ass would've still been sitting in there eating gumbo dinners mixed with hot water made in garbage bags.

We pulled away from the prison in a beat up Buick Century that I suspected was stolen, because the steering column was necked. I didn't give a shit whose car it was, I was just grateful to be on the other side of the fence. Riva was too. She stuck her head out the window to express how happy she was by lifting up her shirt.

"Fuck all you redneck yee-ha mutha'fuckas" Riva hollered like a cowboy, "To all you punk ass C. O's I'm out'a here bitches!"

Riva's cousin Levitra and I just laughed our asses off as Riva flashed the busload of prisoners that were just pulling in to begin their time. The cold blast of air made me feel light headed for a second, because the ventilation in prison was suffocating. I forgot how nice it was to breathe real air.

Off we were to BPT. I hadn't been there before, but I heard Bridgeport was even more dangerous than New Haven. Riva couldn't testify to that either, because she was from Brooklyn, but Levitra lived in Bridgeport all her life and said that it was a complete war zone full of heartless killers and drug dealers.

As soon as we exited the Merritt Parkway Riva had Levitra stop by the nearest gym.

"Yo leave the car runnin'," she uttered before hopping out, "I'll be right back."

At first I couldn't understand why a person would want to hit the gym on their first day out of prison, but about five minutes later I understood the reason very well. Riva came back to the car with like 4 credit cards and a pocket full of cash that she stole out of the women's locker room. She said the dummy behind the desk never suspected that she wasn't a club member, because she had on a sweat suit. The prison grays gave the impression that Riva worked out there I suppose.

Our next stop was the Trumbull Mall. It was only two minutes away from the gym, which gave us more than enough time to speed shop with the stolen credit cards.

"Ai'ight Mende, you hit Macy's, I'll hit Lord and Taylor and Levitra you hit all the sneaker stores" Riva directed, "get as much as you can, because we don't have that much time before they report their shit missin'. If they ask for I.D play it off like you left it in the car, but don't run out the store whatever you do trust me!"

"If you see something cute don't forget my size I'm a 12" Levitra notified me as she handed over one of the platinum credit cards.

"Let's meet back at the car in a half hour and as soon as you're finished throw the cards in the garbage" Riva insisted.

"Aw'right yo."

The six months behind bars destroyed my tan, but being that I looked ghostly pale worked out for me this time. Out of all the stores that I hit not a single employee asked me for I.D. They all assumed that I was just an innocent white girl with good credit even though the name on the card read Kee Jung Kim Chow!

I couldn't believe it when I got back to the car. Between the both of them Riva and Levitra were only able to charge about $500, whereas I alone got away with like $5000 worth of shit. That's when I realized what I had been doing the whole time was wrong. Instead of denying my whiteness, I should have been using it to my advantage. Elvis did it, Eminem did it, and Bill Clinton for example, all surrounded themselves with less fortunate black people to make themselves stand out and look better. At this point I realized that it was time to stop fronting like I was from the hood and start acting more like a white chick. This didn't mean that I still couldn't pull black dudes.

Levitra stopped by a liquor store before driving to her apartment on Hamilton Street. We rushed inside with bags galore then exchanged clothes with each other as we tried on each out fit. While Riva sat on the couch guzzling down the brown juice, I modeled for her in my new satin bra and panties. It felt so good to wear something that actually fit me, unlike those XXL sweat suits and prison uniforms.

"How does this thong look with these low-cut jeans?" I asked Riva with a girly stare.

"That shit is hot, but it can't fuck wit' these stretch Baby Phats I got" Riva shot back. She seemed uninterested in flirting with me for some reason.

"Yo Levitra, call up some toe curlin' pussy knockin' niggas so we can get this party started," Riva hollered into the bathroom, "I was down for thirty months and feel like I could ride thirty dicks!" She laughed

I laughed along with her, but I was insulted that she didn't want me to make her feel good. Here I was thinking this girl was doing favors for me cause she liked me in a sexual way, but Riva hadn't come on to me once since we got out. I wasn't looking for a girlfriend or nothing, I just wanted to know what was up so I could move on.

"I thought you said we were going to get drunk and bug out together...what's the deal?" I whined upset, "why can't we do our thing baby?"

Riva sucked her teeth then got up off the couch while Levitra talked on the phone with some dude. She called me into the other room to talk in private.

"Look here Mende I hope you know that what happened between us in there was only for *in there?* I was bored and you looked lonely, get it? On the brick it's all about the dick, so snap out of it right now. There is no *our thing!*"

After being told nicely that I was just a prison fling, I got mad and tried to change my demeanor to replicate hers.

"I think I'd rather prefer a dick in my mouth than your tangy twat anyway bitch! You ain't all that" I said as I turned to walk away.

"You a muthafuckin lie!" Riva retorted, "I know if I laid on this bed right now you would drive your tongue right up my ass" Riva laughed with a sneer.

She pulled down her stolen jeans and spread her smooth brown butt cheeks apart to give me a glimpse of her pinkness, knowing I could not resist. When I bent down like a sucker with my eyes half closed and my tongue at full length, Riva turned around and slapped the taste out of my mouth. She hit like a dude and that shit stung.

"I was just testing you hoe! Don't you ever talk to me like that again or I'll slap those plastic lips off your face," she hollered while gripping my throat, "now apologize!"

Riva turned me out in prison and she knew it. I felt so stupid. I stood up with the same reaction as if a guy had dissed me and walked out the room.

"Don't you walk away from me girl...get your sweet ass back here and apologize to me!"

Like a lost and turned out trick, I walked back in the room and apologized. I felt like I was in no position to be starting shit, so I submitted to Riva's demand.

"I'm sorry" I said, "I don't know what I'm apologizing for, but I'm sorry Riva okay?"

Riva raised her hand to scratch her head, but I flinched thinking she was going to hit me again.

"Relax Mende...I'm not gonna' hurt you baby...I'm your friend remember?"

Surprisingly Riva tongue kissed me while gripping my butt with both hands, "and if you're good, maybe" Riva whispered in my ear, "just maybe I'll let you eat me out before I leave, but for now keep it on the down low...SSSSHHH."

Riva's split personality made it hard for me to believe her, but when you're confused everything sounds like the truth.

Ten minutes later the doorbell rang. The dudes that Levitra called over showed up. All four of them were tall like professional basketball players and each one of them carried a different brand of liquor in their hands. They took off their bulky leather coats then started talking with each other.

"Yo I got that one right there...*but I seen her first though*," they argued over who would sleep with Riva.

"Then I'll take shorty with the phatty,"

another said, referring to me like I was piece of meat being selected at the market.

"Nah...we sharin' that phat ass son!"

After puffing a few blunts and getting bent out of our minds, Levitra and her boyfriend went into the bedroom. Riva let the dude she was with suck on her breasts right in front of me, while the other two guys stood at each end of the couch.

"Two heads are better than one," they laughed dangling their long dicks in my face.

I was drunk about now. Ten months was the longest I had ever went without having a man up in me, so I had some catching up to do. Since Riva didn't want me, I was going to make it worth my while and do both dudes at the same time. I admit that I enjoyed rough anal sex, however my stuff could only stretch but so far before it started bleeding messing with these King-Kong dong niggas.

The next morning my butt hole felt sore as hell. I took a beating. They ran a choo-choo train in my doo-doo drain. I positioned myself in the shower with my back arched and a cheek spread apart with one hand. With the movable showerhead I sprayed my torn canal with cool water for relief. What happen was Riva got so drunk and passed out in the middle of making out with her jump off and he eventually joined in with his friends. I promised myself that I would never let three guys triple team me ever again, unless I was getting paid big figures.

Scene Twelve:

Hardheads never learn

Just because birds of a feather fuck together, doesn't mean they get along. Riva turned out to be a drug-crazed psychopath that only cared about herself. When we weren't bickering over dick, we were fighting over bags of blow. The credit card and boosting schemes were not cutting it fast enough for the amounts of coke we sniffed and there was no way I could stay cramped up in Levitra's small apartment too much longer.

As if we were still inmates with no ambition to do anything else, Riva and I sat on the couch watching Jerry and the rest of the dim-witted talk shows while we got high. Levitra was getting sick and tired of Riva and I eating up all of her food and smoking all her weed without paying. She threatened to put me out if I didn't get a job, and since I failed my first urine test, my P.O was on my back about finding work too, or I was going to get violated. Levitra kindly informed me that her job was hiring and suggested that I fill out an application, but I never got around to it.

"If you lazy asses don't get up off my couch and get a job today I'm sellin' all the clothes you boosted last week and I'm kickin' both of y'all bitches the hell out!"

When Levitra started running that get a job or get out shit on Riva, she happily packed her bags to head back to Brooklyn. Her welcome was much worn out.

I wanted to hit the city with Riva, but unless I wanted to get violated, I couldn't leave Connecticut.

"If you're ever in New York" Riva licked the cocaine from my nostrils, "look me up" she said, "you might catch me in Yonkers at Sue's Rendezvous."

That was that. Riva hopped on the train and bounced. Levitra gave me exactly one week to get my shit straight or I was out on the street. I swear she got on my last nerve, but I had to kiss her ass until I could find a place of my own. Surprisingly I actually got the job at the bank where Levitra worked. The bank manager thought I resembled his wife in the early years of their marriage and practically hired me before even filling out the application. If my last name wasn't Gubenhimer, I don't think he would have hired me. Most times I dissed older white guys, but I charmed this one to get special treatment. To separate myself from the other birds, I dropped all the slang talk and spoke like an *educated* suburbanite.

Working for the first time in my life wasn't all that bad. All I did was count money and snoop into people's business all damn day. Everything was going fine, until two weeks into the job when this black Expedition with dark tints pulled into my drive-thru window.

At first I didn't think anything of it until the driver laid on the horn like an idiot.

"One moment please" I scowled as I completed the last transaction, "Good morning...how can I help you today?"

The window came down slowly and a shiny pistol appeared. Dirty Roy spoke into the intercom, "If you don't have all of my money by the next time I see you I swear your pale ass is done with!" Then his face and gun disappeared in the tint.

Roy was serious and didn't even give me a chance to make up an excuse this time. He was the only person in Bridgeport that gave me coke on credit and I owed him $700 already. Roy had that good shit. That raw shit that makes your jaw move side to side like Sammy Davis JR. See Riva was supposed to give me half of the money, since she sniffed half of what Roy gave me, but her ass was long gone now and I was left holding the bag.

Here I was making $9.00 an hour and

boosting groceries for dinner and had to pay this nigga too, shit...something had to give. The thought of beating Roy crossed my mind a few times, but he was too deep in the streets to hide from.

"*Where in the hell am I gonna' get $700 from?*" I asked myself.

In the past I always robbed Peter to pay Paul, so somebody was going to get it, know what I mean?

As the next customer pulled up to the drive-thru window I sat there in deep thought worrying about how not to get shot again.

"Good morning Mrs. Goldstein would you like your balance," I snapped out of it.

"Yes I would dear thank you" the old woman replied caressing her mink coat while she waited.

Mrs. Goldstein always deposited at least $4000 into her account every Wednesday since I worked at the bank. When I read that she had a balance of $94,136.07 on my computer screen I almost choked.

"One minute Mrs. Goldstein?" I stalled for time, "our computers are slow today." After reading all her private information I said, "have a nice day," as I sent the balance statement through the air tube.

The entire time I was plotting on how I was going to jack Mrs. Goldstein's old Zionist ass. Being that the cameras were on me, I memorized her home address until I was able to write it down in the restroom. Working at the bank gave me access to all types of personal information and I could also cash stolen checks at will. All I had to do now was figure out how and when to make my move.

On my lunch break I snorted the last little bit of coke that I had with me. 4:00pm finally came around and it was time to punch out. Usually I rode home with Levitra, but she was off today, so I took the city bus to the address I had written down in the restroom. I got off the bus holding the piece of paper in my hand like a tourist, as I walked up and down Park Avenue until I found the right address.

There it was, Mrs. Goldstein's Lexus parked in the driveway. The front door was cracked and all the lights in the house were on. I had to see if the old lady lived alone, before I did anything else. When I peeked through the side window, I heard Mrs. Goldstein talking to her cats then left.

The next night I had Levitra drop me off a block away from Mrs. Goldstein's house. Of course I didn't tell her what I was up to, because I didn't want that nosey chatterbox up in my business.

"I'll see you later Levitra thanks for the ride," I hopped out in a hurry.

"Thanks for the ride my ass" Levitra held out her hand, "I need money for gas girl where you think you goin'?"

I gave Levitra my last $20 then slammed

her piece of shit car door hoping that it fell off in the middle of the street.

Looking suspicious was of no concern to me. In this neighborhood the only camouflage needed was white skin. I must have walked around the block ten times before I moved in for the attack. Given that I only scoped out the place once, I prayed that no one else was in the house, because I didn't have a gun.

Quickly I crept to the back of the one floor ranch style home to make sure it was clear. Mrs. Goldstein was on the phone, so I waited underneath the patio deck until she got off. Every little noise startled me. An ambulance siren in the area set off all the more paranoia. Finally I walked up the steps on edge before ringing the bell.

"Hello...who is it?" Mrs Goldstein merrily voiced from inside.

I took off running. While she went to the front door to see who it was, I ran to the back door again and snuck inside. Mrs. Goldstein was startled half to death when she reentered the kitchen. Her facial expression changed in an instant. She looked at me oddly backing away as I moved forward without saying anything.

"You're that girl from the bank!" She flinched, "What in the hell are you doing in my home! Get out right now or I am calling the police!"

I took the kitchen phone off the hook while approaching with my hands out to choke her.

"You ain't calling nobody," I growled.

"Oh my god!" Mrs. Goldstein stifled, "I-can't-breath..."

"Where's the purse" I demanded to know as I released my grip, "I know you got money."

"Help!" She cried out as soon as I let go, "HELP ME SOMEONE PLEASE!"

For a senior citizen Mrs. Goldstein put up one hell of a struggle. The phone was making that off the hook irritating sound, while she tried to run out the backdoor. I snatched her from behind to shut the bitch up, and then grabbed a rolling pin off the kitchen table. I beat on Mrs. Goldstein's head like a lunatic drummer until she collapsed on the floor.

The flour on the wooden roller absorbed some of the blood, but my hands were dripping with it. Bloody fingerprints seemed to appear everywhere and I began to panic. At first I tried to clean up the mess than said fuck it. I didn't even search the house like I planned. I just grabbed what was in sight. The purse was sitting on the kitchen counter, so I rummage through it with the quickness and I lucked up.

Some people write down their PIN numbers so they don't forget and Mrs. Goldstein happened to be one of them. Her four-digit access code was written on the back of the slipcover that enclosed the card. I didn't have time to go through every little compartment, so I took the whole damn purse, even though I only needed the checkbook.

Before stuffing the motionless body in the closet, I removed Mrs. Goldstein's wedding and engagement rings from her fingers. Hanging up was a full-length mink coat that felt even more comfy than the Chinchilla Duane gave me. It must have been my lucky day, because I also found two winning $50 scratch offs in the pocket.

It was time to split. I backed out the driveway in the old lady's Lex hoping no one heard the screams.

"That wasn't so hard" I thought to myself while standing at a 24 hour ATM counting cash.

Like with most debit cards, for the sake of the customer's security, Mrs. Goldstein's card had a daily withdrawal limit of only $400. My plan was to write out big checks anyway, but I needed some cash to pay Roy. A half hour later I pulled up on the Ave like I was doing the damn thing. As I pulled up in the shiny Lexus, all the niggas on the block nodded to the sounds of Raekwon's Purple Tape..."*Peace Connecticut!*"

"Yo where's Roy?" I asked around as one of his snot nose workers sold me a bag of Dro and two twenties of blow.

"They across the street" the kid answered as he crumpled up the crisp twenties I handed him.

I wasn't really worried about the car, so I left the shit running with the system pumping when I walked over to where Roy was playing cards. I don't know if it was the fur coat, or if I was just nervous, but my forehead was sweating like a pig and it was freezing outside.

"You betta' have my money or that mink is my girlfriend's new grocery store coat," Roy said as his eyes stayed focused on the deck, "I should just take that shit anyway!"

Roy looked upset. Some dude named Cream was ripping his ass in Black Jack for thousands of dollars. I handed Dirty Roy his money before lighting my third cigarette in the last five minutes. Roy didn't even count the cash I passed him. He just started laying bets right away only to lose it all in one hand.

"Get from behind me you're bad luck" Roy barked at me, "*I knew I should've hit that seventeen damn!*"

I walked away before Roy or anyone else took his or her frustration out on me. Customarily if I ever stepped on the block 12 O' clock at night, I was usually looking for one of two things. Drugs or dick or sometimes both. This time however, I just wanted to be by myself. I drove without direction and ended up at Seaside Park, where I smoked myself to sleep.

I was snoring when I awoke to a bright light shining in my face. It was a police officer tapping his flashlight on the glass. Something told me to pull off, but I hesitated.

"The Park is closed ma'am what are you doing here at this time of night?" The officer asked. He pointed his light throughout the car as I let down the window, "Can I see some I.D?"

He probed.

"I'm sorry officer I don't have any on me right now, I think I left it at home."

"What's your name?" The young Spanish cop sighed, "how about registration and insurance do you at least have that?

"Sure. My name is um Sandy...Sandy Goldstein. This is my grandmother's car" I started crying, "I know it was wrong officer, but she doesn't know that I have her car. I snuck out of the house to be with my boyfriend."

At this point I started sobbing like a scared little a girl. I thought I was going down for sure.

"See officer my grandmother forbids me to see my boyfriend because I'm Jewish and he's Puerto Rican...like you are. See I love Carlos and all I wanted to do was see him before he leaves for the Army tomorrow."

I got out of the car and threw myself at the cop, while weeping on his shoulders. I presumed that he was Puerto Rican, because he looked like Mark Anthony without glasses. If he didn't have sympathy for me and my bullshit story I was hit.

"That's terrible" he shook his head appalled, "when I was young I experienced the same racist situation with my first girlfriend. I loved her but her father hated me because I was from a poor Latino section of town...you look like a nice girl Sandy, so I'm not going to run you in. Just be careful and take the car home right now."

The officer walked me back to the car and

closed the door for me. I couldn't believe he went for it. My pouting lips and sad blue eyes did him in. The dumb spic even gave me a tissue before pacing back to his cruiser sulking in his own thoughts.

"*Whew! That was close*" I released a deep breath of relief as I drove to Levitra's.

The next morning I woke up excited. I convinced Levitra that it would be most beneficial to her if she submitted the falsified checks at my drive-up window.

"If everything goes according to plan Levitra, you'll have gees in your pocket and I'll be out of your crib tonight!"

In exchange for Mrs. Goldstein's wedding rings and half of whatever amount of money we scammed, Levitra agreed to play the role. 9:15 A.M Levitra pulls up in my lane like a normal customer.

"Can I help you..."? I acted cool.

"Yes I'd like to cash a check please," Levitra spoke into the intercom.

"No problem ma'am...large bills or small" I said with a straight face.

"The Bigger the betta'!" Levitra's hood voice leaked out.

I ran the check through like I would any other, "okay" I said, "you're all set Mrs. Goldstein have a nice a day!"

Five minutes later we worked the same routine. Levitra made the first check out to cash for $3000 and the second one the same. It was that easy. We could have run this scam until Mrs. Goldstein's account was drained, but after the second trip, Levitra hadn't returned in hours.

I was beginning to think that she ran off with the money, until strangely enough my computer screen shut down. Everyone else's computer worked fine except mine. I looked around the bank and noticed the manager's door was cracked open. He stared at me intently as he spoke on the phone with someone before closing the door with his foot. The lethargic security guard that stood at the door came rushing over to my station soon after.

"Mr. Roberts would like to speak with you in his office right away."

"Why is something wrong?" I acted concerned.

"I don't know. He told me to escort you to his office...lets go."

With a pocketbook strap over my shoulder and keys in my hand, I left my post and followed the rent-a-cop like I was actually going to go with him. Instead, I bailed out the exit as customers entered the bank. Realizing I had escaped out the side door, Mr. Roberts and the fat security guard chased me to the car. I hauled ass out of that parking lot, like I just robbed the motherfucker, flooring it all the way to the highway as police passed me going the opposite direction.

What I didn't know at the time, was that

Levitra had got caught trying to write out a check at some top-notch jewelry store in Trumbull. When the police tried to notify Mrs. Goldstein about the stolen checkbook they recovered, Levitra got scared and snitched on me about everything she knew. One thing led to another and they soon discovered Mrs. Goldstein's body.

Scene Thirteen:

On the run

Instead of ditching the stolen Lexus, I drove to my grandmother's house in Mt. Vernon. At this point in my life I should have learned my lesson and head out to California even if I had to hitch hike, but I stayed on the east coast anyway. Eventually I abandoned the car in the South Bronx, after driving it around like it was mine for a few days.

Until things calmed down, granny Gubenhimer's spot was going to have to do. She wasn't as rich or nosey like my other grandmother in Cali, because she suffered with Alzheimer's disease. There were no rules to abide by at granny's, so I came and went as I seen fit. However on some days granny would forget who I was. If I didn't remind her that I was her son's youngest daughter Patricia, granny would have called the police about a stranger roaming the house.

Conveniently Sue's Rendezvous, the strip club that Riva supposedly worked in occasionally, was only fifteen minutes away from where granny lived. Every other day I stopped by off and on to see if Riva was working, but each time I missed her. During my sixth visit I found a new occupation.

"I'll take a double shot of Hennessy and a Heineken" was the first thing out of my mouth when I hit the bar one day in Sue's.

"I'm sorry honey, I know your new, but we're not allowed to serve the girls when they're working," the petite Spanish bartender replied, "it's policy."

"Oh sweetie, I don't work here," I said while covering my chest a little more, "I'm just looking for a friend. Do you know if Riva is dancing tonight?"

"Riva? Never heard of her, but if your looking for a *friend* I get off at three," the bartender winked and licked her lips before serving me my drinks.

I could see why the bartender thought I was a new dancer, because my attention-grabbing tits bulged through the low cut top I wore. You should have seen the guys swoon at the bar when I removed Mrs. Goldstein's fur coat. It was as if my shirt read *come and get it*. A man wearing a pasta stained tee shirt sat down on the stool next to mine, then slid me a $50 bill as I downed a shot of cognac.

"I heard you say that you're looking for a friend" fatso smiled silly, "how much for a lap dance or a blowjob for that matter?"

It was flattering that everyone thought I looked sexy like the girls on stage, but talking to this guy was not a good look. He was the epitome of a slime ball pervert.

"Since you were snooping in my conversation so hard, you must have heard me say I DON'T WORK HERE ASSHOLE!" I snapped at the depraved son of a bitch before spilling his drink and shoving his money away, "Now leave me the hell alone!"

Next this clean cut Italian guy, who later identified himself as the man in charge, came over to where I moved my seat. He stared down at my thigh as I adjusted my mini skirt to sit down.

"Hey I notice you always come in then leave all the time. Can I interest you in a job? We could always use a pretty girl like yourself."

"Um not really. I was just looking for a friend" I responded more friendly than I did with the last guy, "does the job you're referring to have *blow* at the beginning?" I smiled with conjecture.

"No...I run a respectable place here." The man stated firmly.

"I think I'll stay on this side of the bar for now" I rebuffed his offer.

"Okay, but it's your loss babe. With a body like that, men are gonna' wanna' slide credit cards down the crack of your ass! This is a strip bar don't forget, so take it easy on my customers doll."

"Wait!" I grabbed his arm right before he walked away, "how much money are we talking?"

"A helluva'lot!" He looked me up and down, "who wouldn't pay to see those tits! My name's Sam, step into my office so I can tell you how it works in private."

As we walked into Sam's office we passed his boss, the real owner, in the hallway. He overheard me doubting myself about being on stage.

"You're gonna' knock 'em dead in here beautiful are you kidding me!" The old man laughed as he escorted another newcomer to the exit. When the old man walked back into Sam's office I stuck out my hand to greet him.

"Hi, I'm Mende" I said with a mega-watt smile.

"Kneel..."

"Nice to meet you Neil, I just love your club by the way."

"My name isn't Neil darling, I mean kneel, as in get down on your knees and show me your résumé. Bend over and touch your toes!"

The boss tested out my goods, by inspecting each one of my holes with his shriveled up salami. The next thing you know I'm on stage the following week squeezing half a dozen ping-pong balls out of my ass. All in all I stayed on the lam from the Bridgeport police department, stripping the winter away through spring. I still hadn't run into Riva once, until the popular "Shake Off" contest, where girls from one state compete with one another, on who's got the best wiggles and jiggles.

My stage name was Emmanuelle and up there I was an erotic beast. Men went crazy as other girls tried to compete with me by picking up beer bottles with their pussy, but I was a natural at it. Every Tuesday the spot stayed rammed with music moguls down to local corner thugs, that all spent major paper, but for the shake off it was more crowded than ever. For a negotiable fee the biggest tippers got to pull a string of beads out my ass. Each time my eyes would roll back as I watched with elation. In no time, a cascade of cash would rain down on my booty. *Cha' Ching!*

On my first big night I made over $4000 in tips, which the other dancers said wasn't shit compared to what I could make after the club. I was content dancing and wasn't interested in selling my body just yet. I had already made enough money in three months to finance a used SL 55 AMG Mercedes Benz, which I registered in my grandmother's name.

"Get your dolla's ready!" The DJ announced as I walked out of the dressing room to the music of Rick James Super freak, "Coming to the stage we have a bunny rabbit with a nasty habit...the eighth wonder of the world! Emmanuelle! The human ping pong machine!"

While the crowd clapped their hands in excitement, guess who walked in with a girl on her arm as they took a seat at the bar. Nobody but Riva and her what looked to be lesbian lover. I watched Riva come in from the mirror and she didn't notice me until I turned around.

"Oh shit!" Riva covered her mouth, "that's the bitch I was locked up wit'" I read her lips, as she stared at me with prompt stimulation.

I worked my signature move for her and her friend in the same way I would for two guys tipping twenties. Like always, people crowded around to see me do my thing. They showered me with bills as the oiled ping pong balls slowly popped out my ass one by one. Riva's girl must have been amazed, because her mouth hung wide open. After I finished my set, I came back out to meet and greet the rappers in V.I.P. Then I sat with Riva.

I Just smiled at Riva, "aren't you gonna' introduce me to your sexy girlfriend?"

"Jackie this is Mende, Mende Meet Jackie...now tell us? *How do you fit all those balls up your ass*!"

Jackie had the best low cut fade in the entire bar. I liked her vibe. She was more animated than Riva. We laughed over the loud music and ordered more drinks as we entertained each other's conversation.

"I would have never thought about

stripping if I didn't come in here for weeks looking for you Riva...I thought you said you worked here?"

"I do work here, but I never told you I danced here" Riva grinned as she made a gun shape with her hand, "you know how I get down girl."

"Hey, what'chu doin' after this?" Jackie asked like she was coming on to me, "We got a room in Manhattan what's up? Lets have some fun."

"Actually they got a room," Riva pointed over her shoulder to a bunch of dudes popping bottles, "they invited us, wanna' roll?"

"I don't know" I paused with second thoughts, "my shit's kinda' sore, I been dancing all night."

"Man fuck that shit you comin' wit' us!" Riva demanded, "Dem niggas got doe and we about to get paid! You ain't gotta' fuck nobody."

I left the club with Riva and Jackie around 3:30 A.M. We followed a black Suburban with Pennsylvania plates in my freshly painted pink Mercedes Benz. At 3:20 we pulled up to the telly and parked. The guys were all over us in the elevator, like they wanted to do it right there. Even the hardest looking one got giddy in anticipation of getting laid.

"Slow your roll! Ain't nothin' poppin' off until we see some paper!" Riva announced.

"Money ain't a thing shorty, how much you need to get it crunk?" The driver said as he flung one-dollar bills at us.

It was apparent that we had these dudes wide open. Out of town niggas were always the sweetest to vict, because they were too trusting.

The moment we entered room 112, Jackie and I took off our shirts to distract them. Riva excused herself and went to the bathroom to supposedly freshen up. While all three guys licked and fondled our tits, thinking they had found some freaks to bang, Riva burst back in the room waving a P45.

"Everybody on the muthafuckin' floor" she yelled, "or yo ass is gonna' die!"

"Hold on wait, let's talk about this shorty," one of the suckers pleaded, "I got a wife and kids!"

"Shut up! Get your ass on the floor."

Jackie's breasts hung low as she went through each of their pockets.

"I know this ain't all you got? Where's the rest of it?" Jackie asked the dude crying, before slapping him in the head with his little gun.

"It's over there wrapped up in the towel by the lamp, just don't shoot us!"

"Yo this ain't shit" Riva frowned in disappointment as she undid the towel with about $2000 in it.

"You should've never fronted like you had big chips" Jackie smirked as she placed a pillow to one of their heads, "I wish it didn't have to be like this cutie...POP!"

Riva shot the other two just as fast. We got

the hell out of there without being seen. If them dudes didn't front like they were big time drug dealers, they would have still been alive. For a measly $2000 to split three ways, the whole thing was a waste of my time. I made more money in a half an hour shaking my ass and these two bitches were going to ruin me with their nickel and dime robberies.

The following afternoon we ate hero sandwiches on my treat from the corner store underneath Jackie's apartment in Bushwick. Since it was a bright and sunny day, we cavorted in front of the bodega, chewing and talking as my car radio bumped the latest Nas. Afterwards I drove Jackie and Riva to some grimey looking projects in Red Hook, to meet with the infamous Woman Hood click I heard so much about.

"Don't say nothin' about what we did last night, cause they on some righteous shit" Jackie prepped me as I parked the car.

"Yeah they do the same shit we be doin'" Riva smirked, "but they try to convince themselves that they're helping out the community."

I thought my flashy ride would produce mad attention, but there were tons of other vehicles shining in the projects, none of which were pink though. The conversation grew quiet when we walked over to a group of chicks sitting on the benches.

"Whad'up yo, you're late" Kali looked irritated with Jackie as Jackie sipped on her wine cooler.

"I know. We had some shit to take care of first."

I stood next to Riva looking out of place.

"Whose miss goldilocks?" Kali smirked at me, "you know the rules yo, members only!"

"This is my girl Mende" Riva said as the crew looked on, "we did time together in Connecticut she's cool."

Kali cut her eyes at Riva then said to me, "Excuse us Mende I need to speak to my girls in private, do you mind."

I took a few steps back before Jackie handed over my keys. Across from us were some other chicks uttering racial slurs at me while they sat on the benches. I know they were just jealous so I ignored them.

"Why don't you go wait in the car" Jackie suggested, "this won't take long."

I wasn't scared at all. I walked back to the car like I didn't care about hearing what their little group had to say anyway. I was doing the damn thing. On my way back to the car mad niggas tried to holler at me of course. As I wrote my number down like an author at a book signing, the nappy head girls on the benches looked heated.

"First things first" Kali read aloud as she held the Daily News up to her face, "*Murderous rampage leaves four dead. Witnesses say that two females wearing masks robbed and killed four Brooklyn men over jewelry and drugs in broad daylight. Sources say the assailants drove away in a black BMW with chrome rims and tinted windows. One of the assailants was said to be wearing a large diamond bracelet with the initials WH. If anyone has any information...*" Kali stopped reading and shook her head in revulsion, "which two of you dumb bitches made the paper?"

No one answered Kali, because they knew if they did it would their behind.

"Nobody knows nothin' now huh? When I find out who it was you best believe it won't be pretty! Anyway we gonna' have to chill for a while. Shit is gettin' hot around BK. We need to start branching out of the city."

Kali didn't waste much time talking about how angry she was about the newspaper article. She could see that the group was falling apart, because most were concerned about clothes, ice and cars.

"To remind you that we're one group I want everybody's whip painted pink" Kali pointed over to my car, "like that shit right there."

"Pink? I thought we're supposed to look inconspicuous?" Riva got smart with Kali, "what is this Mary fuckin' Kay or somethin'?"

"Is makin' the front page of the newspaper inconspicuous bitch? It was probably you and one of your cokehead friends that did that hot shit! This way you'll think twice about using each other's registered cars to do stick ups in."

When the meeting adjourned, each

member got in her car and left. Riva and Jackie walked over to my car with five other girls in the Woman Hood that felt more like they did. They could care less about some damn community programs or homeless shelters. Most of them had remained the same rogue group of cutthroats that they were when they were in the Buck fifty crew.

The only ones that seemed to care about continuing the VETS legacy were Ma'ati, Toya and Kali. Kali would never give up on what the Woman Hood stood for. She witnessed Ma'ati get her mother off of drugs, which let her know that what they were doing was worth it. Loony actually ran one their after school programs now.

"Can I live?" An aggravated Woman Hood member spoke out before Riva passed her a blunt, "I'm tired of this shit! Can I do my thing without Kali's permission first! I'm not a lil' kid na'mean?"

"Yo I say fuck the Woman Hood and lets do our own thing" another jeered, "hell yeah!"

As the six unhappy chicks sat around my car expressing their dissatisfaction, I decided to add my little two cents in.

"Why don't you just take what's yours instead of complaining...you got guns, they got guns...do you! You don't need them" I instigated.

Observing the success around my neck and looking at the car I sat in, made them listen to what I had to say, instead of brushing me off like some dumb chicken head that didn't know nothing.

"I think Kali's playing you. Who made her the first lady of Brooklyn?" I questioned sarcastically as I did my lipstick in the mirror, "if you really wanna' get paid I say leave all that righteous shit behind and start your own crew."

"Mende hit it right on the head" Jackie said, "cause guess what? Y'all didn't know that she had a crib in Yonkers with a brand new Porsche SUV in the driveway, did you?" She took me there once when you were locked up, I forgot to tell you Riva."

"Say word!" Riva got excited, "Save the community my ass! I bet you that's where all that money we've been giving up is stashed! Those conniving little bitches!"

Scene Fourteen:
Set you up to wet you up

Following our conversation in Red Hook, Riva and Jackie made devious plans to raid Kali's crib. I was the little voice in their ears causing mistrust and had them right where I wanted. Whenever I got involved in anything I always had ulterior motives and planned my own agenda, while those two schemed on their associates. I decided it was time to head out to California and start living my life like a bona fide white chick. Fuck the hood and all the people in it! Besides my candid outlook on street life, I was also in dire need of a good plastic surgeon, because the ones in New York sucked. I was ready to cross back over, but not before going out with a bang of treachery.

I got Jackie to set up a get-together with Kali, where I would explain this heart felt story about how horrible the sex industry is and how certain people need to be offed. I knew Kali would go for exterminating fresh meat, because her other routine was getting old.

"So tell me Jackie, what's on your mind" Kali solicited conversation as we all walked down the Fulton Street Mall together.

"My friend here has some information that you might find interesting, go head Mende tell her what you told me."

"Well...you would never know by just taking the train or driving to work or simply observing the scene, but there are vampires walking the streets of New York day and night in search of their next prey. They can tell if you're underage or if you're merely out past your curfew looking for some fun. These types of guys are trained to notice the girls who could barely walk in heels or the ones who apply extra makeup just to look older. In the blink of an eye runaways and rebellious girls are taken off the streets then put to work never to be seen by their families again."

"And by telling me this you..." Kali motioned her hand for me to explain my point.

"I know I'm an outsider, but I was thinking that since the word was out on you amongst some circles throughout the city, you might want to chill for a minute and go a different route. I'm a stripper you see, and I know where one of New York's biggest child pornography rings holds its auctions. It's sick! You should see what they do to little girls in there. They videotape guys pissing on kids and all types of shit. Most of the buyers own strip clubs and escort services and every month bands of perverts flock to this spot in Hunts Point in the Bronx. Tonight they're gonna' be swapping, selling, testing and auditioning runaway teens and illegal aliens from all over the world...does that sound like something you'll be interested in ending" I asked Kali.

"Hmmm?" Kali stopped walking and looked me in the eye, "what do you get out of it?" She questioned, "'cause you don't seem to be the concerned citizen type to me?"

"Listen, when I first started dancing one of these bastards raped me. I just want to see him dead...that's it" I answered smoothly.

"Jackie I swear, if this is some bullshit I'm gonna' fuck you up and for you" Kali poked me in the chest, "if you ever double-cross me in any form whatsoever I will track your white ass down and cancel you like a stolen credit card."

"Why would I double-cross you?"

"I don't know? Why do niggas mess with white chicks when they got beautiful black girls at home?" Kali said, "Who knows? All I know is your story better be tight."

The story I told Kali was actually true, there really was a child porn exchange taking place tonight, but I neglected to tell her that Riva and Jackie double-crossed her.

At midnight, I as an honorary member of the Woman Hood, dressed in all black. I parked my Benz around the corner from Club Playpen, a huge strip club in an old factory building. I hopped in the mini van Kali and her crew sat in across the street from the entrance. SUV's and limos were parked on every corner in a three-block radius.

Toya drove another minivan with four girls in it I had never seen before. There were nine of us in total. Kali, Toya, Jackie, Riva and the four I never met. Ma'ati was out of town with her boyfriend Laquan, so she couldn't make it. Lucky for her sweet ass, because death was lurking for the Woman Hood.

"*Is everything all set?*" Toya spoke to Kali on her two-way like a cop, "...*Over.*"

"Roger that...Riva's at the front door now scooping out the guard" Kali responded, "when she comes back we're goin' in."

Tonight's entry into club Playpen was by invitation only, but the oversized doorman seemed to like Riva. He let her in with no problem after so-called patting her down by rubbing his hands all over Riva's soft butt cheeks. From where Kali sat it looked like Riva was enjoying it.

"Riva's flirty ass better not fuck this job up" Kali stated as she sat in the driver's seat looking from afar, "she acts a little too friendly with them grease balls for me."

As Riva made her way through the club she stepped over a couple having sex in the hallway. The music was playing extra loud and each section of the club had a different fetish being acted out. People were fucking and sucking out in the open like a Greek orgy. There were hundreds of girls in there and even more men roaming around. One girl, who looked like she was 12 years old, was getting plowed doggy style, while another guy stood in front of her jerking off. It was crazy in there.

"Look what the cat dragged in," some fat Italian shouted as Riva walked into the most exclusive section of the club, "excuse me gentlemen this one's not for sale."

The room full of Asian businessmen were not interested in Riva anyway. They were there to stock their massage parlors and day spas. While juvenile Asian girls were selected from cages as if they were dogs, the head honcho walked Riva to the exit.

"Is that her across the street in that green van?" He asked.

"Yeah" Riva answered, "and a few more...you got the money?"

For a minor-league price of $5000, Riva and Jackie made a deal with the police. The dirty cops wanted Kali dead for shooting up that dope spot back in Brooklyn two years ago. All Riva and Jackie had to do was bring Kali inside. Riva counted the cash then shook the cop's hand.

"*Make it nice and quiet*" the cop said, "there's a lot of important people in here...rich people, and I don't need any problems, so get them to the back room as quick as possible."

Riva left. She walked out the club over toward the van with a smile on her face. Kali and them were loading their guns as Riva slid the side door open.

"*Yo how many people are up in there?*" Toya inquired on her two-way.

"About two hundred tricks and about twenty guards including the doorman. I think we can take 'em though" Riva said, "but we gotta' act like we're hoes or they're gonna' know something's up."

"Whatever let's go" Kali uttered.

"Wait!" Riva said, "you gotta' leave the guns here cause they're gonna' check us at the door."

"Fuck you we're not goin' up in there empty handed are you crazy" Kali retorted as she twisted a silencer on the tip of her pistol, "I said let's go. If they check us we just shoot our way in that's all."

Kali left the keys in the ignition and hopped out with everybody else.

"*I want you two to stay in the car just in case something goes wrong*" Kali whispered into her two way before she caught up with us, "*if we're not back in thirty minutes come in blazin'!*" she instructed the twins.

Riva and Jackie didn't know that the twins were parked around the corner in a third van. Kali didn't trust us and devised a back up plan just in case, I guess. That's when I got ready to do the dip set on everybody's ass. As Riva, Jackie, Kali, Toya and the four other chicks piled up at the front door, I drifted off from them slowly. I noticed the Twins were double parked two cars down from me, on the already over crowded side street.

"*Damn!*" I said to myself as one of them got out the van.

"Where the hell you goin'" Mika asked with discretion as I went for my keys.

"No where" I said, "I left something in my car."

By now Kali and them were already in the club.

"They're with me" Riva said to the dude guarding the stairs, "we're all performing tonight" she blinked her eye at the bouncer with a pack of cigarettes rolled up in his t-shirt sleeve.

"It's gonna' be the best show ever" Jackie sucked her finger for leverage.

The guard let them upstairs without searching anybody. Kali couldn't believe what she was seeing as they walked passed the different rooms. There were so many naked teenage girls being pulled from one place to another by chains around their necks, it reminded her of the slave trade depictions. Four big black dudes ushered Jackie and Riva in one room and the other four in another.

"Wait here" they said to Kali and Toya as they scooted them into an empty locker room, "we'll be back in a minute."

"Yo this don't feel right" Toya said to Kali,

seconds before the lights went out.

"*Yo get the fuck out'a there now!*" The Twins voiced sounded through Kali's two-way, "*that white bitch just pulled off in your van, it's a set up!*"

I knew if I pulled off in my car the twins would have followed after me, so I blocked them in with the Benz, so they couldn't move their vehicle. I took off in Kali's Caravan head for the Bronx River Parkway.

"*BOOM! BOOM! BOOM! BOOM! BOOM! BOOM! BOOM! BOOM! BOOM!*" Shots echoed on the third floor.

Just like that, four of the Woman Hood chicks were dead. Before the police hit team pulled the same ambush on Kali and Toya, they were greeted with a surprise.

"*ZIPPP! ZIPPP! ZIPPP! ZIPP! ZIPP! ZIPP! ZIPP!*" Kali's silent weapon fired as she laid on the floor shooting at the door.

"*BLOOM! BLOOM!*" Toya let off too.

The two cops were hit. They stood crouched over in the dark hallway holding their stomachs in agony. Kali and Toya burst out the door shooting some more. The light from the barrel of their guns lit up the pitch-black hall like flashing strobe lights. Toya finished them off with one shot to each of their domes.

"Aw' shit they got all of 'em!" Kali yelled out to Toya when she seen her girls lying dead on the floor, "where in the hell is Riva and Jackie!" she hollered over the loud music.

"*POW!*" A shot fired from around the corner.

"I'm hit!" Toya cried out.

Kali reached behind her back. She pulled out two Glock 9mm's and started a flurry of gunfire as she covered Toya. People down stairs didn't know what was going on because the music was deafening. Before Riva ran down the back stairwell exit she fired a few shots at Kali.

"*What'chu want us to do? Riva and Jackie just came out the back! Where are you?*" Nika voiced through Kali's two-way.

"Upstairs! We need help! Toya's hit!" Kali responded, while firing at the people shooting from the staircase.

It was either follow Riva and Jackie or help Kali and Toya. The twins grabbed the HK assault weapons from the backseat. They ran to the same door Riva and Jackie came out of to rescue their friends.

I wish I could have seen Riva's face once she noticed I had left her ass hanging. While Kali and them were getting dealt with inside, the plan was for me to wait outside for Riva and Jackie. Instead of all of us going to Kali's hideaway home in Yonkers to take her doe, I felt that three was a crowd. It's called betrayal. Why would I care about some bitches I barely knew?

Before agreeing to be a part of Riva's little plan, I made sure Jackie showed me exactly where Kali lived in Yonkers. I got off the Bronx River Parkway on the Oak Street exit. Time was short. I had about ten minutes to get in Kali's crib, get out and make it to the airport before my scheduled flight for 3 A.M. took off.

Instead of kicking the door open, I busted the large glass bay window with a rock. Inside I found a shoebox of cash with a note on top.

"*Save for S.E.E.D.S*" the reminder notice read in Kali's handwriting.

By the way Jackie described the Woman Hood's finances, I knew I would find much more in Kali's crib if I looked long enough, but I had to make it quick if I wanted to catch my flight to California. I finally learned my lesson that greed can get you killed.

When it was all said and done, 19 people got shot and killed at Club Playpen, including four Woman Hood members and six off duty police officers. The other nine were not so innocent bystanders that got in the way when the twins burst in spraying anything that moved. When the real police arrived, numerous arrests were made for all types of reasons.

The only one out of the Woman Hood that got knocked was Toya. Jackie and Riva disappeared and the twins took off down south. By the time Kali put two and two together, I was in first class sipping on iced tea, enjoying the best air travel money could buy.

Scene Fifteen:

Karma

Not a day went by when I didn't think about my wild street life experiences. Almost two years passed with no problems, but technically I was still a fugitive wanted as a murder suspect in Connecticut. I changed my entire demeanor and even married this college geek my sister had introduced me to. The guy wasn't that cute, but he had money, so I said what the hell when he asked me to marry him. Tying the knot was actually beneficial, because I had a new last name. As a wedding present Jenny let us have her beachfront condo for almost nothing. She was moving into a huge mansion with her new boyfriend, some rich investor from the Bay Area.

Adjusting to my new drab lifestyle was hard, but I managed. Instead of driving a flashy car, like the pink Benz I had, I now drove a white Volvo "soccer mom" station wagon. There were no Baby Phat jeans or any other hip hop outfits hanging up in my closet and I didn't wear jewelry that much anymore, either. All I wore now were prissy dresses from Talbot's and loose dungarees from Ann Taylor. Taking my husband's advice I let my behind even out to its natural flat shape, instead of getting more butt implants. He thought big booties were disgusting. However he loved the big tits, so I kept them for his sake.

To pass the time I joined a local knitting club that met on the beach once a week. It was boring as hell, but hey, it beat sitting in jail or lying in a casket dead. No one in the knit club was a native to California, they all seemed to be from out of state. It made me wonder if any of these women moved out here to hide their promiscuous and shady past as I did.

...Like I said in the beginning, I had been suffering with the same nightmare for two weeks straight. I kept denying my intuition that Kali was on my trail, but I could feel it. When we returned to Santa Monica from our honeymoon in the Caribbean, my husband noticed that our propane grill was smoldering as we pulled into the driveway.

"Gee hun...*that's odd*" he frowned, "maybe our neighbors used it and forgot to turn it off?" He thought about it optimistically.

While he walked around the side of the house to check it out, I stayed in the driveway unloading the car.

"Honey can you help me with this bag? It's heavy." I called out for him, but he never answered.

My husband was like a kid. He loved to play hide and seek and usually jumped out from somewhere to scare me. I prepared myself for a surprise as I carried the small luggage into the living room.

"Hun-ney...where are you?" I played along.

When I sat the bags down on the floor my heart dropped to my feet. Kali was sitting on the sofa with her shoes off holding a gun to my husband's head. She had made burgers right before we pulled up.

"Well, well, look at miss thang dressed like the American housewife" Kali stared with a slight smile, "is that one of your stripper costumes or are you a rehabilitated hoe now?"

My husband looked at me in confusion.

"Oh she didn't tell you hun-ney?" Kali laughed in my husband's face, "Your wife used to slide Heinekens up her ass for a living before she decided to steal TWO HUNDRED THOUSAND FROM MY HOUSE...ain't that right Mende?" Kali lowered her voice.

"Mende? I thought your name was Sally?" My doofball husband asked.

"You should really get to know someone before you marry them, buddy. Her name is Patricia Gubenhimer, aka Mende, the white trash bitch from Wallingford and she's wanted for murder in Connecticut. I know because I've been tracking her triflin' ass down for a year and a half." Kali said.

"How'd you find me?" I wondered.

"Your dumb ass left a little black book in the Benz glove compartment with all types of phone numbers and addresses in it" Kali stated with joy then scowled, "so here I am...because of you, seven of my friends are dead...you been a naughty girl Mende" Kali turned her gun on me, "I came to take what's mine."

"What do you want!" I yelled, "your fucking money! You can have it!"

"No. This ain't about the money. I want payback bitch! I WANT YOUR FUCKIN' LIFE!"

Before Kali could shoot, my husband struggled with her. She elbowed him in the face before chasing me into the kitchen.

"I tried to be nice to you" Kali argued with my husband when he grabbed her from behind again, "but playtime is over son!"

"BANG!" Kali shot him and he dropped like a rock.

"Did you actually think you could get away with that shit Mende?" Kali yelled out as she searched each room.

My heavy breathing increased as I tried to hide around the corner holding a knife for protection.

"BANG! BANG!"

"AHHH!" I screamed.

Kali shot off one of my tits as they poked out around the corner wall I thought I was hiding behind. I fell to the floor bleeding as the saline bags oozed out my chest. In the travails of my mischief I laid there thinking about what my father once said to me. *"You're gonna' learn one day that Niggers ain't nothin' but trouble Patricia!"*

Kali stood over my body watching me bleed to death.

"Game over Bitch. Time to go to hell!" Kali placed her gun between my eyes and fired. I guess my father was right after all.

THE END

Read bonus chapters of

Payback's A Bitch

the first episode

Starring Cream and War with special guest appearances by Ma'ati and Kali. Two wrongs don't make a right, it makes it even!

IN STORES NOW!

Scene Fourteen

People sat inside the funeral home for hours listening to community sellouts speak the bullshit, while others mourned the loss of their family member and comrade. Even War had tears in his eyes thinking about his older brother who was also shot and killed by police in the P.T Barnum housing projects when he was 11. The entire service was crowded with black people from all over the area. It was a sad event of course, but most attendees were more angry than sad. This was the area's third shooting this month of an unarmed black man killed by police.

Reverend Budsac spoke to the mourners about how most police officers were actually good guys and that it was a sin to have animosity toward the officers who shot these young men. Ajax's father stood up in awe of the Rev's outrageous eulogy. This was the same Reverend Budsac that sniffed on the low and was known to have "relations" with many of the ladies in his congregation. Nobody was trying to hear the crap the Rev was putting down, so the crowd started to get loud in objection.

Cream and Warren paid their respects. They viewed the body then consoled Ajax's parents as they passed by the front row. Ajax's mother was more than vexed that her son lay dead in a casket because some hotheaded trigger-happy rookie decided to fly off the handle. She had blood in her eye like *George Jackson*, shaking in her seat boiling with anger. The more the Reverend spoke, the more people began walking out to take their dissatisfaction elsewhere.

Besides those that worked with the crooked police department, people of all nationalities living in the area couldn't stand cops because they seemed to always start shit. The largest part of the police force that patrolled the streets didn't even live in Bridgeport. They were mostly from the suburbs and viewed black people from how they're portrayed on the big screen or television.

Tension was brewing outside. Between all the dirty shootings and political corruption the local media had recently exposed, tempers were on the verge of explosion. Two officers with a K-9 riding shotgun drove by the service slowly and one of the asshole cops motioned with his hand like it was a gun, pointing his finger out of the window as the dog barked unremittingly.

"Yo did you see that muthafucka' try to mark us!" a person in the crowd hollered.

Seconds later the wake turned to furor after shots were fired at the cops by one of Ajax's grieving friends. The police shot back into the air and people scattered all over the place, some running out of the funeral parlor before they even got to pay their respects.

Warren moved out of the way as a group of young kids ran passed him down the block. He stood out front of Pettway's Variety to warn Bing-O that the Police were on their way down the block. Bing-O was talking to Geek on a payphone about somebody he was planning to victimize.

Cream watched the commotion from inside the car waiting for War to return from the store. Being that vehicles had them blocked in he couldn't move the car until everyone else pulled out. Warren strolled back to the car smoking a loose cig with a bottle of beer in his hand.

"Who was shootin' yo?" he asked nonchalantly.

"I don't know" Cream replied, "whoever it was dipped down Baldwin."

They weren't going anywhere no time soon cause the police were shaking down mourners as they exited the service and the parking lot was still packed. A rusted Toyota Corolla parked next to them had a 14-year-old in the back seat with his head tilted back, looking up at the drooping upholstery. All Cream saw was a woman's head bopping up and down.

"Oh shit, that looks like Miss Tucker," he uttered after recognizing the woman in the car.

Warren straightened up in his seat to see what Cream was talking about. The young trick handed the woman two loose fraggles (crack rocks) before she got out, spitting semen on the ground.

"Damn when she start cluckin'?" War stated, as if he was missing out on something good.

Cream acted like he didn't notice Miss Tucker when she looked at him by turning his head the other way.

"*Tap Tap Tap*!" Miss Tucker banged on the window glass.

"Hey baby, how we doing today" she asked,

"you boys want yo ding dongs sucked? I'll do ya' nice and good. Roll down the window so I can talk to you for a minute baby."

Cream let the window down backing away as Miss Tucker tried to kiss him on the cheek.

"What do you want Miss T, does June know you're out hear actin' like this?" Cream said, blowing up her spot.

Miss Tucker widened her eyes when he mentioned her son's name. She was high as a kite and up until now, she hadn't recognized her former fifth grade student.

"Uuh, I wanted to ask you if I can borrow ten dollars," she asked while scratching her chest and the side of her neck, "cause um, they're gettin' ready to turn my lights off and um, I need to see if I'm gonna' correct homework papers."

Cream knew she wanted to buy more drugs, so he dissed her ass. Before Miss T left she asked them again if they were sure that they didn't want to have a good time with her. After getting the message that nothing was happening, she walked away tapping on another car window to pull the same stunt.

"Damn, what the fuck happened to us? That lady used to be one of my favorite teachers in grade school," Cream revealed.

"Crack happened nigga!" Warren cheered, "that's why I only sell drugs to white people now, cause that shit got muthafucka's around here buggin' the fuck out! Plus they be broke. Yo I heard some base head stabbed Biffy over one slab yesterday."

"I'm telling you son, we don't need that energy in our circle. And don't sleep either...white people steal entire continents. What makes you think they won't kill your ass over a couple of grams?"

Cream was determined to convince his a-alike, that he should leave the street grind behind him. He wanted to use the money he already accumulated doing dirt for something more virtuous. Warren played along with Cream hoping to skip another one of his boys exhausting lectures.

"Maybe we can set up a basketball clinic for the young dudes who love to ball," Warren thought out loud playing the role.

Cream's thoughts were far from that. He was thinking on another level.

"Please!" Cream reacted insulted, "how many niggas they got in the NBA right now?"

"A lot," War estimated.

"Then tell me why do so many NBA cats set up basketball centers in the hood, when they know it's one out of a million that actually make it to the NBA? Wouldn't it make more sense to establish something more people could succeed in? How in the hell can you come off with one in a million odds!" Cream articulated.

He wasn't far from the truth. Most athletes and entertainers that came from the hood rarely built a foundation that had an overwhelming impact on the lives of black people.

"I don't care what kind of job you got, if you sign a contract you're agreeing not to bite the hand that feeds you. Peep how all the athletes and actors that made power moves, got shut off like light switches soon after."

"You might be right on this one" Warren

addressed, "look what happened to Jordan when he dissed Nike and tried to retire. His pops mysteriously got kilt...c'mon a car jacking in the middle of the fuckin' desert!"

"Bill Cosby's son was supposedly jacked too don't forget," Cream recapped, "when he tried to buy 'The Little Rascals' and NBC. Something mysterious like that even happened to Dr. J's son?"

It was time to bounce. Conspiracy theory time was over. The jam-packed parking lot emptied and they were finally able to pull off after sitting there for forty minutes.

"About time!" Cream yawned, "My ass was starting to stick to the seat. Does the AC ever work in this bucket?"

Warren paid Cream's jokes no mind and kept rolling down the window. He didn't care what anybody thought about his car cause he had a different one every other month. The Maxima that he drove was a chop shop special that only ran him $1000. In high school War had hooked up with this oily Arab mechanic that traded luxurious stolen cars teens brought him, for somewhat legal shoddy style rides, which were basically vehicles made out of stolen car parts with phony paperwork.

The Avenue was getting flooded. Everybody from Ajax's wake started to hang out on the sidewalks. It looked like a Freaknik meets Bike Week had taken over the Ave. Girls were everywhere and players were stopping their cars to rap to every chick out there.

"You see that chick in front of the Jackson club?" War pointed.

"Who the one with the mean stance talking

to Dirty Roy?" Cream confirmed.

"Yeah. I keep seeing her everywhere I go," Warren sounded perplexed, "the first time was in Tipton's a couple of months ago and then she started poppin' up all over like she's following me?"

"Whoever she is, somebody's hitting her pockets off with all types of loot or she hit the lottery? Would you take a look at that fuckin' Benz!"

The mysterious woman they were referring to was Kali, a new chick on the scene that had that "rich bitch I'm the wife of a don" look. Mad cars and trucks were pulling over and beeping at Kali making an effort to get with her, but she dissed them only giving the top drug dealers the time of day. Warren continued to drive slowly the entire time he was talking. He paid no attention to the cars that were honking behind him to speed up.

When he circled the block, he slowed down even more just to get a better glimpse of Kali who was leaning on her pink SL 55 AMG Mercedes Benz. It was fully hooked of course with 22-inch Benetto rims gleaming, TV and navigation system in the steering wheel and all that. Kali winked as Warren drove by staring at her ride.

Cream requested that War stop by his house before they went anywhere else so he could change his clothes and strap up, given that so many strange faces were in the area. War was talking to someone on his cell and momentarily said to Cream that he would park around the corner, since there were some youngsters riding dirt bikes up and down the street doing wheelies and tricks. It was only a hop skip and a jump for Cream to walk to his spot anyway, so it wasn't a problem.

Cream crunched glass as he walked confidently in his dress shoes stepping through the narrow path that led to his aunt's house. The dogs barking were nerve racking, but there was something more threatening and odd. Geek was standing on the back steps of Cream's aunt's house peeking into the kitchen window. The demented looking white boy turned toward him with a .22 in his grip after hearing Cream accidentally kick a tin can. Cream knew what time it was now, but what he didn't know was how he was going to escape without getting shot. Before he could turn around to jet, Geek let off two shots in his direction.

"Get your ass over here! Where you think you going nigga?" Geek yelled, firing another shot.

Panicking because his gun was still in the house, Cream cut ass back down the narrow pathway. The whole time he just knew he was definitely going to get it in the back. Keenly reacting he lunged through a piece of dry-rot plywood that barricaded the entrance to an abandoned garage. The fiends inside the garage dropped the needle they were sharing, looking just as nervous as Cream was as he crashed to the floor creating a large dust cloud.

Seconds before Cream dove inside, Geek fired two more shots, which ricocheted off the outside of the garage. No sooner than Geek could get off another shot, a loud ear popping blast went off.

"BLLOOOOMMMM!" Echoed the sound down the path like thunder.

"AARRHH MY GOD! My leg! Ahhhh! My fucking leg!" Geek yelled intensely.

Uncle Raymond had let loose his 12-gauge Mossberg from the top balcony. It overlooked the backyard and pathway, which gave him a clear shot. In excruciating pain, the cornball assassin limped away on one leg. He hopped past the garage where Cream lay on the ground unnoticed with a 2X4 in his grip ready to swing. When Warren heard the shots he rose up as if he was sober. He grabbed his loaded 9mm from under the seat at the same time that Cream ran out into the street pointing and yelling. For a brief moment he had his gun pointed at Cream then lowered it.

"Get that nigga Yo! He tried to take me out" hollered Cream, as Geek hopped toward the get away car.

In a flash Warren floored the gas crushing Geek between his car and theirs. Like a trained hit man he then let off his entire clip into the passenger side window and Geek's body at the same time. The driver had one hand on the wheel, hanging half out the car with all types of fluids gushing from the side of his head. The entire ordeal seemed to last an eternity, but actually went down in less than a minute.

After the first shots were fired no one was in sight to witness Warren and Cream speed off down the block. Whenever there was a shoot out in the hood, people of all ages knew the drill, stop and drop. Another rule of wisdom was you didn't see shit...even if you witnessed everything.

Scene Fifteen

"**Y**ou, hit yo?"

"Nah I'm straight," Cream answered War out of breath.

He advised him to slow down so they didn't look so obvious fleeing the scene. Warren cruised passed Newfield Park like nothing even happened.

"I don't know what made that kid think he could come to the East End with a little ass twenty two. What the fuck was he thinking?" War stated hyped up.

"I should have known something was up when Unk told me some white boy came by the house lookin' for me," Cream exclaimed.

There were spent gun shells all over the car. Some stuck between the seats, a few in the utility tray and even some on the dash.

"Let's get rid of the heat right now...drive by the bridge and I'll toss it," Cream suggested.

"Fuck it I don't care, that shit got bodies on it anyway. What I want to know is who let off that cannon?" Warren wondered.

"I'm pretty sure that was Unk," Cream affirmed, "His pump is loud as hell. When I heard that shit I thought somebody blew up a quarter stick of dynamite!"

"Yo, Uncle Ray is 'bout it 'bout it," War

laughed.

As they rolled over the bridge, Cream tossed a handful of shells and War's 9mm into the Yellow Mill channel. The adrenaline rush was still pulsating. Cream was engrossed in the thought of almost losing his life, while Warren drove down East Main St. War offered Cream a cigarette to calm his nerves, but he declined.

"I gotta' get out this damn suit" Cream complained, "I almost bust my ass sliding in these slippery ass shoes."

He showed Warren the bullet hole in his sleeve, grateful that it was the suit that had the hole in it and not him. After stripping down to his undershirt Cream decided to head downtown for some new gear. Warren agreed to patronize Halls sportswear, a black father & son business, only reason being was that Cream said he would treat. Cream always made the effort to support black business whenever possible, instead of handing his money over to others so easily.

Warren on the other hand thought that a white person's ice cubes were colder than a black person's ice cubes and would happily dump piles of cash into their registers just for the sake of being white. Of course if you're a white retailer that automatically makes your merchandise "official" Warren thought.

When they got downtown it was flooded with people shopping like it was the first of the month. After paying for both of the throwback jerseys as well as both pair of jeans and fresh pairs of city's, they left their suits in a dumpster outside of the Arcade mall.

Before they got in the car Warren spotted

another glimmering pink Mercedes. This one was a G500 SUV with New York plates too but had Ma'ati getting into it.

"Yo ain't that shorty over there son?" Warren uttered, while lacing up his new feet.

"Let's try catching them at the light."

War pulled up behind the G5 at the stoplight. He beeped the horn three times as the truck pulled off. Four blocks later and tired of beeping, he decided to pull along side of them in the on-coming traffic lane. The chinky eyed sista' pushing the Benz hollered out the window like Warren was an idiot.

"Take a picture next time asshole!" she screamed, "It'll last longer muthafucka'!" Then she sped off.

Ma'ati recognized Cream waving his arm out the window and asked her sister to pull over. Michelle pulled to the curb and Cream carelessly crossed the street walking over to the passenger side.

"Raheem are you crazy?" Ma asked.

"Yeah what's up with your friend driving like he don't got no sense! He almost caused an accident driving on the opposite side of the road," Shell snapped.

"Could you please follow us, we have to talk about some real shit," Cream claimed.

Ma'ati smelled liquor on Cream's breath causing her to frown. By the look in his eye she could tell that he was serious. With uncertainty Shell agreed to follow. Warren led them all the way down Fairfield Avenue crossing the city limits into a cheesy motel parking lot. Michelle complained somewhat, sucking her teeth like she wasn't feeling the situation.

"Got me up in some motel parking lot. I just know these niggas don't think they're gettin' some coochie?

"Shell that's all you think about" Ma rebuked, "Raheem jus' wanna' talk, that's all. I haven't seen him in awhile and I wanna' hear what he has to say."

Cream was in the motel office talking to the sleazy manager for a couple of minutes then came out waving everyone into a first floor room. When Warren stepped out of his car, Michelle liked what she saw and changed her disruptive tune.

"Now that's what's really good," she muttered.

Warren had a squint in his eye, thinking the same thing as he watched Michelle stride gallantly toward them. He bit down on his lip wondering how many licks it would take to get to the center of that?

Michelle's look was primetime, replicating that of her sister's striking beauty.

"Would you relax nigga," Cream mumbled, "at least wait until she gets into the room before you start droolin'."

Ma'ati, Michelle and their cousin were on their way back to Manhattan for the weekend. Ma'ati reassured her younger cousin Twana not to worry about any funny business, because she had *Prometheus*, her .380 pistol and her razor on her person. It was Friday and all three females looked vibrant, scowling as they entered the musty motel room.

"Welcome to Chump Plaza ladies...do not make yourself at home," Warren announced as the girl's walked in.

Shell was the only one who laughed at his corny jokes. Cream instructed the trio to make themselves comfortable for the time being. Warren inhaled a deep breath as he got a closer look at Michelle's mouth-watering cleavage.

"*Those things can't be real*" he thought, making eye contact with Shell who now had her legs crossed sitting on the edge of the bed. Twana, the youngest one of the three, lit a cigarette talking like she was grown.

"Cut you short nothing! Why y'all got us up in this raggedy ass motel room," she loudly voiced.

Cream didn't know where to begin. He gave Ma'ati a tight hug expressing how happy he was to see her and conveyed how much he was sorry about the misunderstanding they had the night she slammed the door in his face.

"I think you could be in danger," Cream warned, "one of Jack's flunkies tried to get at me today and I just thought you should know."

Like always, Warren cut in the conversation before Cream could finish.

"They were waitin' for my nigga" War disclosed, "they might try to see you too nah'mean?"

Cream sat down next to Ma on the bed bypassing his blabbermouth friend.

"It might not be safe staying in your building right now. I know you're a tough woman and all, but I don't think you should be alone with Jack's crew on the loose. If you let me, I'll protect all of you Ma...from head to toe."

Ma'ati smiled at her sister on the low. Shell and Twana started raising their voices in concern after Warren kept talking.

"What did you get her into? who is trying to kill you Tiara? Wait 'till daddy finds out!"

War looked at Cream then Cream looked at War, "Daddy? That's your sister?" They asked in unison.

"Yeah that's my nosy ass sista' Michelle and this is my lil' gully ass cousin Twana."

"I'll be that, but I ain't little," Twana squeaked, "I'm sixteen you betta' recognize," she said palming her breasts.

Although one would think Twana was in her twenties from the way she dressed, her true age showed from the way that she acted. Ma'ati got up and sat down between her sister and Warren. She noticed how much Shell was sweating Warren's sex appeal and whispered in her sister's ear.

"You two should get along really well cause you love salad and he loves tossin' it."

Michelle nervously squirmed from the delightful thought. She sat wondering which way Warren licked, *"Side to side, clockwise or counter clockwise?"*

Shell had to start asking questions to change the subject, re-crossing her legs to extinguish her sudden burst of horniness.

"So tell me Warren, somebody tried to kill you?"

"Yo you should've seen it" Cream cut in this time, "after my uncle just about blew the niggas leg off, War did a Swartz-a-nigger shootin' shit up like a ghetto Terminator!"

Cream laid it on thick and it was obvious to everyone in the room that he was trying to hype up the story. After hearing the exaggerated version,

Michelle asked Warren about the real story. While the two started talking amongst themselves, Ma'ati pulled Cream into the small bathroom so they could have more privacy.

"See man, that's why I got so mad at you that night. You could get me killed doing dumb shit like that. I still don't really know what you and Action Wackson were tryin' to pull off, but that's one of the reasons why I moved out of Brooklyn. I had to get away from the bullshit niggas pull."

Cream moved her close to him trying to explain everything.

"You could ask War, I didn't even know those niggas. I never saw those kids before in my life. I'm not gonna' act like I'm a drug dealer when I'm not. Look sweetness, I just wanted to tell you that you could be in danger. I don't want anything to happen to you, cause I really like you nah'mean? You don't even know how much you've altered my consciousness already. Something activated inside of me that I can't explain. Just give me a chance."

"I have no time to play games" Ma'ati clarified, "but what you need to do is stop thinkin' about us and call your uncle to see what the deal is at home. I'm happy you're okay and I must admit that maybe I over reacted that night...I'm feeling you too and usually when that's the case, the man turns out to be an asshole."

Ma'ati kissed him on the cheek then went back into the room with everybody else. Cream thought calling the house was a good idea, so he stayed in the bathroom dialing his cell.

"Sup Whodie?"

It took Cream a moment to recognize the voice, since he hadn't seen or heard from his southern cousin Tymel in years.

"Who is this?" he asked.

"Yo cuzin Tymel, nuck'ah."

"T-Y! What's the deal...when you break north?"

"I flew up with moms yesterday. She wanted to surprise you, but hold on cuz, pops wants to speak with you."

Uncle Ray got on the phone.

"What in the hell took you so long to call? I didn't know if you were hit or what. You okay boy? I just watched the live local news and they said those two had it coming anyway. I doubt if the police push a strong investigation cause those fools were wanted for murder and armed robbery they're damn selves. They strangled some old lady last night robbing a bodega" Ray said, "their mug shots were just on the news a minute ago. You ever heard of Omar Watkins and Earl Simsbury?"

Cream didn't know Geek's government name was Earl Simsbury, but he knew the driver Omar Watkins.

"Yeah I know his ass" Cream was sad to say.

"When I seen that ugly face staring through my window I almost had a shit hemorrhage. I was so pissed I wanted to chase him with the butter knife I was using on my toast."

Ray did most of the talking while Cream listened. After he finished telling old war stories Cream asked Unk if he would look in his bottom drawer and put everything that's in it into the gym bag sitting by his bed.

"I want you to take out like $3000 for yourself" Cream said, "leave me ten and hold the rest while I'm gone and oh yeah, can you put it in my truck for me too? There should be a extra set of keys on top of my dresser."

That was cool with Ray. You didn't have to tell him twice. If Cream asked Tymel to do something, he would probably still be on the phone explaining how and why. Ray would never give Simone the lowdown because she would have a fit and some things are best kept between men. Gunshots went off in the area daily, but this time since they sounded so close telling her what happened would only add stress.

"Tell Auntie I called and that I love her. Just say I went out of town and that I'll be back next week. If my mother calls tell her the same. You always come through for me Unk. I owe you one."

Ray didn't ask any questions at all before he hung up the phone. Twana knocked on the bathroom door after Cream hung up.

"I hope you didn't blow up the bathroom cause I got to use it," she said through the door.

"Now? I'll be out in a minute," Cream griped.

"Not now, but like right now. Open up."

Cream was taking a quick leak, but Twana opened the door before he was finished like she didn't care.

"I told you I'll be out in a minute" Cream huffed zipping up his jeans.

Twana was trying to see what he was doing and getting her peek on at the same time. Cream came out the bathroom pointing his thumb over his shoulder at Twana then shared the 411.

"You'll never guess who the driver was," Cream said staring up at the ceiling.

War didn't look too puzzled, but acted interested in knowing anyway.

"Mutha-fuckin' Bing-O," Cream divulged.

"Get the hell outta' here, Bing? I knew something was up with that cat." War laughed, with that sinister look in his eye.

Michelle seemed bored. She said she's had it with guys acting like they were gangsters all the time and was looking for something different.

"Yeah right Shell," Twana blurted after flushing the toilet.

Cream got everyone's attention.

"This is what we're gonna' do," he said "I gotta' stop by my crib for a minute to get something. Then we're goin' to Ma'ati's spot so she can get a few things if she wants."

"We are?" Michelle inserted.

"Obviously" Ma'ati sighed, "we can't stay here Shell, if it's okay with you can Cream stay with us at your place tonight?"

"Can Warren come too?" War slipped in for himself.

"I don't know, I guess...but does this mean we're not going out like we planned?" Shell asked, a little irritated.

"Lets go then, it really stinks up in this rat hole," Twana complained, as if her number 2 odor didn't add to the room's mildewed funk.

"We out."

BUY

Payback's
A
Bitch

a novel by
MARCUS SPEARS

TODAY!

WHEREVER BOOKS
ARE SOLD

Coming in 2005

Son of

a

Gun

a novel by
MARCUS SPEARS

Get it when it drops.

ORDER FORM

Address to:
4Word Press P.O Box 6411 Bridgeport, Connecticut 06606

www.4wordpress.com

PURCHASER INFORMATION

Name:_____

Inmate #:_____
(necessary for institution orders)

Address:_____

_____

City: _____State: _____Zip:_____

Total Number of Books Requested:_____Payback _____Behold

Payback's A Bitch $12.00 (SALE PRICE)

Behold A Pale Whore $12.00 (SALE PRICE)

Shipping/Handling $3.00
(Via U.S Priority Mail) (ADD $1.00 FOR EACH ADDITIONAL BOOK)

<u>**TOTAL**</u>_____$15.00

For orders being shipped directly to prisons costs are as follows:

Payback's A Bitch   **$11.00**
Shipping/Handling   **$3.00** (add $1 for each additional book)

Accepted forms of payment include:
Institutional Checks or **Money Orders <u>Only</u>.**
(no personal checks please)

<u>**TOTAL**</u>_____ $14.00

PRICE & AVAILABILITY SUBJECT TO CHANGE WITHOUT NOTICE

ORDER FORM

Address to:
4Word Press P.O Box 6411 Bridgeport, Connecticut 06606

www.4wordpress.com

PURCHASER INFORMATION

Name:_____

Inmate #:_____
        (necessary for institution orders)

Address:_____

_____

City: _____State: _____Zip:_____

Total Number of Books Requested:_____Payback _____Behold

Payback's A Bitch $12.00 (SALE PRICE)

Behold A Pale Whore $12.00 (SALE PRICE)

Shipping/Handling $3.00
(Via U.S Priority Mail) (ADD $1.00 FOR EACH ADDITIONAL BOOK)

TOTAL_____$15.00

For orders being shipped directly to prisons costs are as follows:

Payback's A Bitch   **$11.00**
Shipping/Handling   **$3.00** (add $1 for each additional book)

Accepted forms of payment include:
Institutional Checks or **Money Orders <u>Only</u>.**
(no personal checks please)

TOTAL_____ $14.00

PRICE & AVAILABILITY SUBJECT TO CHANGE WITHOUT NOTICE